WITCHING FOR HOPE

PREMONITION POINTE, BOOK 2

DEANNA CHASE

Copyright © 2020 by Deanna Chase

Editing: Angie Ramey

Cover image: © Ravven

ISBN print: 978-1-953422-00-2

Bayou Moon Press, LLC

www.deannachase.com

Printed in the United States of America

Hope Anderson loves her life. She has a great business that's thriving, the best friends a girl could ever have, and a coven she can count on. Oh, and she's been single for over fifteen years and likes it that way... until the love of her life, Lucas King, walks back into town and throws everything she thought she knew about herself into chaos.

If that wasn't enough, now her mother is in town to warn her about a curse that happens to all the Anderson women when they turn forty-six, and she isn't talking about hot flashes or mood swings. But maybe the curse isn't so bad, because now there's someone distributing dangerous drugs in their quaint town and Hope's going need that curse to bring down the drug dealers and save everything she loves about Premonition Pointe. The question is, will Lucas prove he deserves to be traveling that line with her, or will she walk away the same way she did fifteen years ago?

CHAPTER ONE

"*I*'m going to need more wine," Hope Anderson said after draining her glass. The early autumn breeze off the California coast blew her dark curls into her eyes, temporarily obscuring her view of her two coven mates, who were grinning at her on the other side of the campfire they'd summoned. It was their monthly gathering on the cliff overlooking the Pacific Ocean where they drank wine, laughed, and cast intention spells meant to help them with whatever life had handed them at the moment.

Unfortunately, they'd already told her they wouldn't help her spell her ex back to Boston, and for that, she was still a little bitter. "If you aren't going to help me with Lucas, how about we do something about this?" She waved a hand, indicating her appearance. "I don't think I could handle it if I found another wrinkle tomorrow morning."

"Sure. Let's do it." Joy was the first to stand, holding out her hands to her two friends. "You lead it," she told Hope.

Hope clasped hands with both of them and started to chant. "Goddess of the sea, hear my wish. Smooth my edges,

1

cast me in gentler light, wash away ten years of time with the shimmer of the moon."

A sparkle of magic cracked through the air, lighting up the night and disappearing just as quickly.

Silence filled the air, just as it always did after they summoned a spell. But after a moment, both of her friends started to giggle.

"Oh, no. What happened?" Hope asked, praying she hadn't turned herself into some sort of Facetuned freak.

Grace Valentine snickered as she refilled Hope's wine glass. "If you could see yourself right now, you'd be cackling your ass off, too. Wouldn't she, Joy?"

Joy Lansing grinned and tied her long blond hair up into a makeshift bun. "She'd probably be in hysterics. I don't think I've ever seen a spell backfire like that before."

Hope glanced down at herself and frowned. Her jeans hadn't ripped at the crotch, nor had her flowy blouse turned into a see-through mesh crop top. "What are you two talking about? The spell didn't work at all. I asked to look ten years younger and yet, here I am in what I'm sure Lex would call 'mom jeans' and a blouse that, while pretty, was purchased to hide those extra pounds I've been carrying around for the last decade."

"It's not your clothes." Grace pulled a small compact mirror from her purse and handed it over. Ever since she'd started dating a man a decade younger than her, she'd started wearing more makeup and more stylish clothes that showed off her curvy frame. Hope had always thought her friend was pretty, but lately, she was looking like a knockout.

Hope paused for a moment before holding the mirror up. But when she did, she let out a gasp as one hand flew up to her hair that had suddenly transformed to the exact same haircut she'd had roughly ten years ago. A haircut and color that had left her horrified and unwilling to leave the house for a whole week before she'd been able to get it fixed. Her previously long, dark curly locks were now cut in an uneven angled bob and were highlighted with blond streaks. "Holy witch balls!" Hope jumped up and started to pace. "This was not what I meant when I said I wanted to look ten years younger."

"I still can't believe you never actually got your money back for that tragic cut," Joy said, shaking her head sadly. "You should've gotten a refund *and* trauma pay."

Hope sat back down and covered her head with both hands. "As if it wasn't bad enough that I've gotten myself roped into working with Lucas, now I have to do it looking like a tragic model from the cosmetology school." *Lucas King*, Hope thought and nearly sighed. He'd walked back into her life a few weeks ago, and ever since, she'd been completely off her game. There was no doubt in her mind that the reason the spell had gone bad was because Lucas had returned to Premonition Pointe and completely effed up her mojo just by being there.

"We can fix it," Grace said, moving to sit next to her friend. "We can cast a reverse spell. If that doesn't work, we'll get Lance over at Liminal Space to work his magic."

Hope stared at her gorgeous friend's wavy auburn hair and scowled. "Easy for you to say considering you look like you just stepped out of a shampoo commercial."

Grace just shook her head and chuckled. "This isn't the end of the world. It's not like you gave yourself a bad case of acne or accidentally hexed someone with genital warts like I did when my magic was out of control. This is just a haircut. Come on, stand up. Let's see what we can do."

"Why not?" Hope said, getting to her feet. "It's not like it can get worse, right?"

"You probably just jinxed yourself," Joy said, pulling three pillar candles out of her bag of tricks.

"Nah. I trust you two." Hope stood and held her hands out to the side as her two coven sisters did the same.

Maybe while we're at it we should spell Paul with an erection so that I can finally get laid.

"What?" Hope stared at Joy. She could've sworn her tall, willowy friend had just said she wanted to spell her husband, except her lips hadn't moved.

"Huh?" Joy asked, her eyebrows pinching together. "I didn't say anything."

"I thought you just said you wanted to spell Paul so that you... um, could get some action," Hope blurted and then laughed as her friend's eyes went wide under the moonlight.

"I... um, I didn't say that," Joy stammered, her expression bordering on horrified.

Grace let out a bark of laughter. "I can't imagine Joy saying that, but it's not a bad idea. I mean, at this point, it couldn't hurt, right?"

"So you didn't hear her say anything?" Hope asked Grace, wondering if she was losing her mind.

"Nope. But what do you say, Joy? Should we give it a try?" Grace asked with a sly grin.

"I don't... uh, wouldn't that be wrong?" Joy glanced away from her friends, but then quickly focused on both of them again. "But really, what's the worst that could happen? He gets an erection? That's not really a bad thing, is it?"

"I'd say it's a really good thing," Grace said. "Come on. Let's fix Hope's hair, then give you something to work with later." She winked at Joy. *Maybe Owen should take Paul to the adult toy store and introduce him to that flavored lube he found or something more exciting like nipple clamps. Something to jolt him out of his sex drought.*

Hope gaped at Grace.

"Oh, come on. I'm not suggesting we alter his anatomy. Just put a little juice in his tank," Grace said, sounding exasperated.

"Nipple clamps?" Hope asked.

Grace stared at her for a long moment, and then she pursed her lips and asked, "Hope, are you reading minds now?"

"Wait a minute," Joy cut in. "You're reading our minds?" She clasped a hand over her mouth and gasped. "You *are* reading our minds. What the hell, Hope? How long has this been going on and why didn't you say anything?"

"I..." Hope shook her head. "I have no idea what is happening." She peered at Grace. "You did just think that Owen should take Paul to the adult toy store, right?"

Grace nodded. "I sure did."

"Something about flavored lube and nipple clamps?"

"Yep."

"Oh, goddess. How do I stop this? I don't want your dirty thoughts in my mind," Hope said, sinking back down onto the log she'd been sitting on earlier. "This could be a nightmare. How? Why? I've never heard anyone's thoughts before. Is it some sort of full moon thing? Did someone curse me?"

"Whoa. Calm down." Grace moved to sit next to her, putting an arm around Hope's shoulders. "You've never heard thoughts before?"

"No. Have you?"

Grace shook her head. "Nope. But I'd never cursed

anyone with acne or genital warts until last month either. Did you know I accidentally made Bill's pants split right down the middle a couple of days ago?"

"You're joking," Joy said, her eyes wide.

"Nope. I ran into him at a house showing, and he tried to take credit for all of my success. All I could think about was that he was showing his ass… again. And the next thing I knew there was a loud split. The best part? He was going commando." She sputtered with laughter and wiped at her eyes as she gasped in a breath. "His client made a quick retreat, leaving mine as the only bidder on the house, instead of the bidding war we'd anticipated. She got a great deal."

"Is that ethical?" Joy asked. "Cursing the competition to get a better deal for your client?"

"I didn't do it on purpose!" Grace insisted. "It just… happened. That's the point. Hope isn't listening to our thoughts on purpose either. The question is, can she control it? So far, I haven't been able to completely control my revenge spells. I just get angry and think something, and the next thing I know, I've given the office jerk acne." She shrugged. "I'm trying to work on having more charitable thoughts, but sometimes things get away from me."

Hope groaned. "Please don't let this be permanent. As much as I love you guys, I really don't want to hear things about your sex lives."

Grace chuckled while Joy grimaced and then buried her face in her hands. When she finally looked up, Joy turned to Grace. "Nipple clamps? Seriously? Is that what you and Owen are up to?"

"No," Grace said with a cackle. "But if I were you, I'd give it a try. I mean, seriously, Joy. You deserve a sex life. Just because you've been married for nearly thirty years doesn't mean you should be regulated to the sidelines."

Joy sighed. "I'm willing to try anything. I just..." She shook her head. "I don't know what the problem is. Paul has never been an every-night kind of guy, but I could usually count on at least once a week. This past year has been drought city, and he won't even talk about it."

"Well, let's give him something to talk about." Hope jumped back up to her feet, waved at her friends to join her, and then snapped her fingers. The candles came to life, flickering wildly in the evening breeze. Hope raised her hands to the sky and said, "Goddess of the sea, hear our desires."

Joy and Grace repeated her words.

"Let the power of the wind and sea reverse this youth spell and return my locks back to their natural state."

Magic zipped around the circle twice and then coiled through Hope's hair just as it had earlier. After a few seconds, it vanished just as the candles went dark.

"Did it work?" Hope asked, tentatively.

Grace and Joy shared a concerned glance.

"It didn't. Did it?" Hope asked, reaching up to touch her hair. It was definitely longer, but it also felt fuller, wilder, as if she'd forgotten to use product or try to tame it in any way. "Oh, no."

"You did say to return it to its natural state," Grace said.

"I didn't mean... oh never mind." Hope dug a hair tie out of her pocket and went to work, trying to tame her out of control curls. "I'll make an appointment with Lance first thing."

"Probably a good idea," Grace agreed. "Now, let's work on

that spell to bring the magic back to Joy's bedroom, shall we?"

A half hour later, once they'd conjured a spell to help Paul get it up, Grace and Joy hugged Hope goodbye and went home to their men. Hope stayed behind and stood at the edge of the sea, staring out at the crashing waves. At midnight she'd turn a year older. Normally she'd take that in stride. Hope wasn't afraid of getting older. She embraced life. Except this year, she had Lucas to deal with. And every time she saw him, all she could think about was what her life would've been like if he hadn't walked out on her... twice.

She let out a grunt of frustration and tried to forget she had to host the open house for Lucas's new store, Against the Grain Interiors, the next evening.

It was going to be the worst birthday in years.

The wind whipped up around her, blowing her out of control hair back. And as she stood there, she heard the wind whisper, *He's here. If you embrace what's offered, your life and everyone else's will be changed forever.*

CHAPTER TWO

"*H*ope? Is that you?" Angela Anderson called out as soon as Hope walked into her cute turquoise blue cottage.

"Nope. It's Betty White. Better put out the good china," Hope said, rolling her eyes. Who else would it be? Hope lived alone... or had until her mother had moved in a week ago. Hope still didn't know how long she was staying.

"Funny." Angela strode in from the kitchen, wearing a rhinestone tiara and carrying two champagne flutes. Sometime over the past two years, her mother had let her long straight hair go natural. It was now a gorgeous silver that Hope already knew she hadn't been blessed enough to inherit. "Happy forty-sixth, baby!"

Hope took the flute, clinked the glass against her mother's, and downed the liquid. "Thanks, Mom." Without missing a beat, she brushed past her mother, intending to move into the kitchen, but stopped in her tracks when she heard her mother's voice in her head.

Everything is about to change, bunny.

Turning, Hope eyed her mother suspiciously. "You knew about this?"

"Knew what?" Angela asked flippantly, obviously pretending ignorance.

Hope stared into her mother's dark eyes and said, "Mother, don't mess with me. What did you mean 'everything is about to change'?"

"So you did hear me." Angela gave her a curt nod, plucked the empty flute out of Hope's hand, and took a right turn into the kitchen.

Letting out a breath of frustration, Hope followed her and leaned against the counter as her mother refilled the glasses and sliced a couple of pieces of double chocolate cheesecake.

"Come," Angela said, bringing the champagne and dessert over to the breakfast table. "Sit. Let's celebrate your birthday."

"I'm not in the mood to celebrate," Hope said even as she took her seat and picked up the fork.

Her mother chuckled. "Okay. No celebrating."

Hope stared at the woman who'd raised her and could barely tamp down her irritation. Angela Anderson had been a single mother who'd worked hard to make sure Hope had everything she needed, including the opportunity to go to college. On paper, she was a great mother. Except, the minute Hope turned eighteen and enrolled in college, Angela had taken off, leaving Hope on her own. What was frustrating was that she came back to Premonition Pointe every few years, acted as if she'd never left, and tried to tell Hope how to live her life. And Hope was certain that whatever her mother wanted to talk about was going to be the same old tired script.

You need adventure, Hope. Fall in love with someone other than Lucas, Hope. Live your life or you'll regret it, Hope.

Hope groaned. She didn't want to hear it. Not now. Not again.

"This isn't a life lecture, bunny," Angela said, giving her a tiny smile. "We're past those now."

Hope blinked. "Did you just hear my thoughts?"

"What do you think?"

Irritation made way for pure frustration, and Hope scowled at her mother. "Don't do this. Not now. Earlier this evening I heard both Joy and Grace's thoughts, and then just now, you seemed to speak directly into my mind. I have zero patience for games. Just tell me what's going on."

Angela placed both of her palms on the table and pursed her lips as she nodded slowly. "I didn't just come home to celebrate your birthday."

"Okay." Hope leaned back in her chair and crossed her arms over her chest. "So why are you here? Are you opening a new business? Met a new guy? Or woman?" Hope's mother had dated across the spectrum of genders. Her only consistency was that none of them ever lasted longer than a few months. Other than the fact that Hope only dated men, she and her mother had a lot in common when it came to their love lives. Nothing ever lasted.

"No. I'm here to help you with the transition." She gave Hope a small smile.

"You mean menopause? 'Cause if so, I think I've got a handle on things," Hope shot back, tired of the runaround her mother was giving her.

"Not quite, bunny." She ran her fingers along the bottom of her chin. "You might want to get the tweezers out before you head to bed tonight."

11

Hope couldn't help herself; she touched her chin and grimaced. "Thanks for that. Super helpful."

"I'm always looking out for my girl."

"If only that were true," Hope said dryly.

Angela let out a sigh and leaned forward. "It is true, Hope. There's a reason why I've kept my distance, and it's not because I didn't want to be here."

"You don't have to explain." The truth was that Hope didn't want to hear her mother's explanation. For a long time, Hope had been resentful that her mother cut out of Premonition Pointe, leaving Hope on her own at such a young age. But she'd mostly put all of that behind her and just accepted that her mother had different priorities.

"Hope," her mother said, sounding exasperated. "I'm trying to tell you something important. It's about you suddenly hearing your friends' thoughts."

Hope blinked, momentarily stunned. Then she placed her elbows on the table and leaned forward. "Okay. You have my attention."

"Three months before you turned eighteen, I turned forty-six and was afflicted with a family curse passed down from my great-grandmother, Moira Anderson." Angela closed her eyes for a moment and then gulped down some more champagne before continuing. "Every Anderson woman in Moira's line suffers from the curse right before she turns forty-six years old. Apparently, it was a spell gone bad that no witch has been able to reverse."

Realization dawned on Hope. "You mean we've been cursed with telepathy?"

Angela nodded. "For me, it's uncontrollable. I hear the thoughts of almost everyone, and it's overwhelming. It's gotten a little easier to manage in the past few years, but I still can't block out the thoughts of people close to me."

She's been reading my mind all these years? Holy mother of the goddess, Hope thought.

"That's why I left," Angela said quietly as she stared at her untouched piece of cheesecake.

A rush of anger surged through Hope's body, and she stood so fast that her chair toppled over. "You've not only been able to read my thoughts, but you didn't tell me. And then you left, making me think… oh, hell. Never mind what I thought." She threw her hands up and hurried from the kitchen, heading straight for her room. There was no way she could talk calmly with her mother. Not right then. Not when she felt like her insides were being ripped apart. Hope spent twenty-eight years thinking her mother had abandoned her. And every time they were together during all of that time, Hope had resented her mother, no doubt thinking terrible things she'd never say out loud, and her mother had heard it all.

"Hope! Wait!" Angela called as she rushed after her daughter.

"Why should I?" Hope spun around, her body shaking from the turmoil racking her emotions. "You kept this to yourself for twenty-eight years. Why do you want to talk now?"

"Because I want to help you navigate this." *I don't want you to suffer like I did.*

It was her mother's thoughts and not her words that sucked all the anger out of Hope. Her shoulders slumped, and she pressed a hand to her forehead as she made her way into the living room and took a seat in her oversized chair.

Angela sat in the corner of the couch, perched on the

edge with her hands clasped together. "I owe you an explanation."

"I think that's an understatement," Hope said, curling up into herself and side eyeing her mother.

There was silence between them for a long moment until Angela finally said, "I'm sorry, Hope. I know what my silence did to you. My only defense is that I wanted you to live a normal life, one that didn't revolve around this curse for as long as possible."

Hope's frown deepened. "I don't get it. What would've been the harm in telling me? At the very least, I'd have been prepared when I started hearing my friends' thoughts."

Angela stared at her nails as if they were the most interesting thing she'd seen in ages. "You don't understand. I knew the curse was coming before it happened. My grandmother told me after you were born. I spent seventeen years stressed about what this would do to my mental state and my relationships. My grandmother Rosie was convinced it was the reason my mother died young. Her death was ruled as an accident when her car went off the road, but Rosie wasn't convinced. Mom didn't handle hearing other people's thoughts well."

"She thought Grandma Mary drove off that cliff on purpose?" Hope asked, horrified. She'd heard the stories. Her mother's mom had gone out in a storm, supposedly for milk and eggs, and had never come back. Except Harriet, their longtime neighbor, said she'd never understood why because there was a gallon of milk and a full carton of eggs already in the refrigerator that evening. Harriet knew because she had stayed with Angela that night after she'd gotten the news about Mary's accident, and she made Angela breakfast the next morning.

"Yes. She was certain of it, but she let everyone think it was an accident to preserve the family name." There was disgust on her face, making Hope question her mother's relationship with her grandmother for the first time.

Hope knew Angela hadn't had a great relationship with her own mother, but she'd thought she was close with Grandma Rosie. *Is that why things were so tense all the time? Did Mom blame her for the curse?*

"No, bunny. I didn't blame her, but I was angry at Grandma for a long time for not being honest about what happened," Angela said, sounding sad. "The truth is that I was angry at everyone for a long time. Everyone except you. It killed me to leave here. But I need you to understand that once I started hearing people's thoughts, it was overwhelming. I couldn't shut them out. It was all the time. I needed to live alone for my own sanity and for your privacy. The last thing I needed to be hearing were the private thoughts of my eighteen-year-old daughter."

Hope stared at her mother with her mouth open as she thought through what kinds of things her mother had heard in her mind. At eighteen, Hope had been head over heels in love with Lucas. They'd been dating for about six months, and he'd been her first for almost everything... *oh, hell,* she thought and felt her face heat with embarrassment. She could only imagine the thoughts and images that had been going through her mind.

Angela nodded. "You needed your privacy. I needed to give you that gift while dealing with my own mental health."

Hope narrowed her eyes at her. "Why didn't you just tell me? Maybe then I wouldn't have spent the past twenty-eight years resenting you." There was no reason to not voice what

15

she was thinking. It was just starting to sink in that her mother would hear her thoughts anyway.

"I was trying to protect you. I didn't want you to go through the anxiety and turmoil that I had. Why tell you and let it take over your life before it kicked in? I wanted you to lead a normal life that I didn't get to have. I did it to help you."

Help? Did it help that she'd thought her mother abandoned her? Did it help when Lucas left and she felt like there was something wrong with her because the people she loved most kept leaving her? She stared at her mother, seeing her pain reflected back at her, and she knew her mother was reading her thoughts.

Tears filled Angela's eyes, and Hope knew she should say something. Anything to acknowledge that she understood her mother hadn't meant to intentionally hurt her. That while she didn't agree that it was better to keep the truth from her, Hope could at least understand her mother's reasons. But she couldn't force the words out. Instead she just felt numb.

"I can't do this right now." Hope pushed herself out of her chair. "I just... I need to process."

"I understand." Angela reached out and grabbed Hope's hand and squeezed it lightly. When Hope didn't return the gesture, Angela let go and sighed. "I'll be here when you're ready to talk."

Hope nodded once and disappeared into her room.

She leaned against her bedroom door and closed her eyes, wondering if there was a spell for turning back time. Just a few weeks ago she'd been perfectly happy with her life. She'd been casually seeing a man who'd wanted the same thing she did—to have a good time. No commitments. No expectations. Then Lucas had walked back into town and she'd suddenly lost interest in her fling. And now her mother was there, ready to talk for the first time ever. It was too much, and both Lucas and her mother were wreaking havoc on the life she'd created for herself just by being in Premonition Pointe.

"Nope," she said, shaking her head. "Not today. Not tomorrow. And not next week." It didn't matter why they were in town or if she could read minds now. She wasn't going to let them or anything else knock her off her game. After fishing her phone out of her pocket, she hit Benji's number.

"Hey, gorgeous. Long time no talk," he said.

Hope could hear the smile in his voice, and it put her at ease. Benji was a cool guy, and she always had a good time when they saw each other. "It's been a little busy here. What about you? I haven't gotten a call either."

He chuckled. "You know me. Just following the waves. I spent the last few months in Hawaii. But I'm back now." His tone was flirty and suggestive.

"Are you free this weekend? Saturday night?" she asked.

"I'll pick you up at seven."

"I'll be waiting." Hope ended the call, expecting to feel more like herself. Instead, all she felt was a faint sense of unease. "Dammit," she muttered and flopped onto her bed, scattering the mountain of pillows.

CHAPTER THREE

*H*ope whipped her Toyota Highlander into the last available parking spot and then ran a across the lot through the light drizzle to the Liminal Space Day Spa. After watching reruns of Golden Girls until two in the morning, she'd finally fallen asleep and woke up twenty minutes after the spa salon opened. After some serious begging, Lance had agreed to fix her hair but only if she came in right away.

"I'm here," she called as she rushed through the door.

Lance, who was busy giving Gigi Martin a blow out, turned and let out a gasp so loud it was audible over the blow dryer.

"Oh, stop. It's not that bad," she cried, bringing both hands up to pat her runaway curls.

Gigi met Hope's gaze in the mirror and grimaced. Gigi was relatively new in town. She'd left her abusive husband and purchased one of the haunted houses Grace had been tasked to sell when she first started working for Landers Realty. Gigi was dressed in a white sundress and had sun-kissed skin. Her honey blond hair practically glowed, making Hope feel even more like a swamp creature.

"Crap. It really *is* that bad, isn't it?" Hope slumped over the front counter, hiding her face.

"Don't worry, Hope," Lance said soothingly. "You've come to the right place. I'll turn you back into a swan."

She glanced up at the big beautiful black man and gave him a weak smile. "You've got your work cut out for you."

"Oh, honey. If I can turn a six-foot-four drag queen with a five o'clock shadow into a supermodel, then there's no need for you to worry. I'll tame those curls and take care of your whiskers."

"Whiskers?" Hope squeaked.

He tapped his chin and then winked at her. "It happens to the best of us, darling. But that's why you're here. Uncle Lance has got you covered."

"Whiskers?" Hope heard Gigi ask him, and she took a seat to wait for her turn in the chair.

"It's nothing you need to worry about, Ms. Gigi. At least not for another ten years or so." He went to work on styling her hair, and ten minutes later, he helped her out of her chair.

Gigi moved with the grace of a ballet dancer toward the front counter. She glanced over at Hope. *Great skin. I wonder what products she uses.*

"Hazel's Witching System," Hope said automatically.

Gigi blinked at her. "What?"

Hope repeated herself and added, "My skin routine. You asked about it."

"I did?" Gigi gave her a strange look and then let out a nervous laugh "I honestly didn't realize I said that out loud."

Oh, hell. She probably hadn't. But since Hope didn't want

to disclose that she'd just heard another person's thoughts, she just shrugged. "You can get it at the health food store a few blocks up."

"Good to know. Thanks." Gigi smiled at her. "Good luck with the hair. I'm sure Lance will work his magic."

"From your lips to the goddess's ears," Hope said.

"You don't need to worry about that," Lance said as he waved Hope over. "I don't know what happened here, but by the time you leave, you're not going to even recognize yourself."

Too late, she thought. Ever since she'd started hearing people's thoughts, she felt as if her mind had been snatched and replaced with a defective unit.

These witches and their beauty spells. I'm amazed her poor hair didn't fall out.

"My hair could've fallen out?" Hope exclaimed and then slapped her hand over her lips.

Lance walked around the chair Hope was sitting in and stared her in the eye.

You can hear me.

She nodded, still covering her mouth.

"Well, *that's* interesting," he said, looking amused. "This is a new development, isn't it?"

Another nod.

"So, what's the juiciest thing you've heard that no one would want to say out loud?" he asked as he ran his hands through her hair.

Hope let out a bark of laughter. "I'm not going to tell you that. I already feel like a creeper just hearing things I shouldn't."

He raised one eyebrow at her. "You didn't tell Grace and Joy?"

"I didn't have to. One of them thought it," she said, chuckling.

"Now we're getting somewhere." He lowered the chair and held his hand out to her. "Come on. We need to condition this mess before we get started."

Once Hope was situated at the shampoo station, Lance waved an assistant off and got to work on shampooing Hope's hair.

"Was it Grace or Joy? It was Joy, right?" Lance asked.

Hope chuckled and let out a contented sigh as his fingers massaged her scalp. "How did you know that?"

"Grace is an open book. Joy is more reserved. You know what they say about the quiet ones."

"Yeah. You're right. But I'm not telling you. That's between her and Paul."

Lance snorted. "Paul. Now he's a real piece of work, isn't he?"

Hope's eyes flew open. "What do you mean?"

He shrugged. "Just that he doesn't seem to appreciate what he has. Joy deserves better."

Hope was on the verge of asking what he meant by that, but then she heard his next thought.

Damn, girl. You did a number on this hair. Gonna have to cut off a lot to salvage it.

"Cut it off?" Hope exclaimed. "How much?"

Lance glanced down at her. "You really do read minds. I'll have to be sure to keep my thoughts PG."

"I don't care about your dirty thoughts," she insisted. "I want to know what's going to happen to my hair!"

"Relax, Anderson. I'll give you a sexy new cut that will have Lucas begging to take you home tonight."

She closed her eyes again and silently cursed him for

bringing up the love of her life. It had been a whole hour since she'd thought about him. "He can beg, but it's not going to happen."

"Uh-huh." Lance couldn't have looked more skeptical.

"Believe what you want," Hope said. "That's over and has been for years."

"Whatever you say." Lance finished with the shampoo and conditioning and led her back to the salon chair. "Now, let me work my magic. Any requests?"

She stared at him in the mirror. "If I tell you to just work your magic, can you promise me when I leave here I'll be as sexy as I was fifteen years ago?"

Lance chuckled. "Hope Anderson, you're already sexier than you were fifteen years ago. You've got age and wisdom and character that have turned you into a badass businesswoman. But yes, I promise that if you just turn me loose, that when you leave here today, you'll feel sexier than you did fifteen years ago."

A chuckle bubbled up from the back of Hope's throat. "You talk a good game, Lance. I'm not sure I believe you, but let's do it. Make me gorgeous."

"I'll do my best."

Lance got to work, and thankfully any new thoughts he had were drowned out by a hair dryer that was in use by another stylist.

An hour later, Lance pulled the drape off of Hope's shoulders and spun her around to see her new look in the mirror.

Hope let out a gasp of surprise. Her dark curls were indeed shorter, but he'd cut it into a sexy bob that was shorter in the back and longer in the front. "You made me look gorgeous."

"Nah. That's all you, sweetheart," he said with a flirty smile. "I just did a little maintenance. Are you ready for that waxing?"

She nodded and followed him into the back where he handed her off to Carrie, one of his longtime estheticians.

"Hi, Hope. Nice to see you again," the tall woman with long dark hair said. She smiled at Hope, but it didn't quite reach her eyes, making Hope wonder what was wrong. Carrie was one of those perpetually happy people, and it was highly unusual to catch her having a rough day.

"You, too. It's been a while. You have your work cut out for you."

Carrie gave her a small smile. "No worries, I've got you covered. Lie down here on the table and we'll get you fixed up. Lance says you need a chin waxing."

Hope nodded. "You might as well do the lip and eyebrows, too."

"You've got it." Carrie went to work with her torture wax, and when she was done, she eyed Hope. *If I can talk her into getting her brows and eyelashes tinted, that would be enough for rent this week.*

"Let's do it," Hope said, wanting to ease the worry in the woman's eyes.

"Do what?" Carrie asked, frowning.

"Oh, um, the works. You know, whatever you can do to spruce this up." Hope waved a hand around her face, trying to cover for accidentally answering the woman's private thoughts.

"Ah. Got it." This time when Carrie smiled, her blue eyes twinkled. "I was just wondering if you'd be interested in tinting your eyelashes and brows. I could also do a facial if—"

"All of that sounds great." Hope had heard the relief in the woman's voice when she'd said she wanted more services. There was no doubt she was under financial strain, and whatever Hope could do to alleviate her worries, that's what she'd do. It didn't hurt that she'd be all sparkling and new for the open house at Lucas's store that evening either.

"Perfect." Carrie got to work, waxing, tinting, and using a bunch of products on Hope's face. When she was finally done, Hope figured she must've taken at least five if not ten years off of her face. "Okay. Your eyelashes and brows are good to go. But the rest of your face might be a little red for a couple days. The waxings and facials can do that sometimes, but then after twenty-four to forty-eight hours, you'll look like a new woman."

Hope swallowed a groan. Of course.

CHAPTER FOUR

*H*ope stared in the mirror and wondered if it would be unprofessional to wear a bag over her head. When Carrie mentioned there might be some redness for a couple of days, what she must've meant to say was that Hope was going to look like a roasted tomato. Whatever she'd used for that facial definitely didn't agree with Hope's skin.

After dabbing on some more makeup, Hope pulled her bangs over one eye, opting to let her hair hide as much skin as possible. It was better than the bag option at least.

"Hope?" Lucas called. "Are you back here?"

"Coming." She walked out of the bathroom and down the hall to Lucas's office. She found him leaning over his desk, reaching for something. And dammit, his backside was really filling out his jeans. She leaned against the doorframe, just taking in the view. She deserved that much at least, right?

"Have you seen my order book?" he asked without looking back at her.

She couldn't help it; she grinned. Lucas had always had

a knack for sensing her presence. "It's at your front counter. I put it there in case you get any special orders tonight."

Lucas straightened and turned to look at her. He'd been busy in the back sanding a credenza when she'd arrived to start prepping his store for the open house. His black and white speckled hair was sticking up in random clumps, and there was sawdust covering his T-shirt and jeans. "Ah, that was good thinking. But I need to check a note." He moved toward the door, glanced at her, and smiled appreciatively. "The new haircut looks great."

Hope's insides lit up with the compliment, and she automatically raised her hand to touch her silky curls. While the facial had been a mistake, Lance had made her hair look better than ever. In addition to a great cut, he'd also used some sort of product that made the curls soft and shiny all at once. "Thanks."

"And happy birthday. I hope it's a good one." He winked at her and swept back into the showroom.

Hope's heart swelled with the knowledge that he'd remembered, and she followed him almost as if he were a magnet. The draw to him was still just as potent as it had been when she was eighteen. Only back then it had been exciting, and now she was just unsettled. He'd broken her heart twice. If she let him in again, she was certain this time it would end up shattered.

Stop it, Hope, she silently scolded herself. There was no point in thinking about Lucas that way. She'd already vowed that she wasn't going there again. She just needed to get through the night, and everything would be fine.

She walked back into the showroom and checked the buffet of crab puffs, shrimp, and salmon bites.

"Where's the beef?" Lucas said from right behind her, making her jump.

"Holy shit," she said, pressing her hand to her chest. "I didn't know you were standing there."

He pressed his hand to the small of her back and reached past her for a shrimp.

"You didn't have any input on the menu, so I just went with a seafood theme. If you want beef, next time I'll—"

"The seafood is fine, Hope," he said with an easy smile. "It was my lame attempt at a joke. Forget it. I should stick to woodworking."

Hope just stared at him, dumbfounded. Then, when his words finally sunk in, she let out a cackle that turned into a full fit of laughter. When she finally got herself under control, she wiped at her eyes and asked, "Did you really just make a joke about that old commercial from back when we were kids?"

He shrugged, and his lips turned up into a sexy half smile. "It got you laughing didn't it?"

"Yes, but I'm laughing at you, not the joke."

Lucas's smile widened. "Whatever it takes to put that sparkle in your eyes, Anderson. It's been a while since I've seen it."

His words sobered her, and she moved to the end of the buffet, pretending to check the napkins and paper plates.

Lucas cleared his throat. "I'll be right back. Going to clean up."

"Yep. I'll make sure the doors are open at six," she said, checking her phone to make sure she hadn't missed any messages. As part of the open house, she'd invited a number of local businesspeople who might be interested in his woodwork. The list included interior designers, realtors, and even a wholesale buyer for an upscale online furniture store, as well as the lifestyle reporter from the *Premonition Pointe News*. If any of them had questions, she wanted to be available.

If there was one thing Hope knew how to do as an event organizer, it was how to create buzz and opportunities for connections. And that was exactly what she was going to do for Lucas.

Because if his business is successful here, he won't leave. Hope scowled at her traitorous thought. She did not need to be thinking of a future with Lucas. That was just not going to happen.

There was a knock at the door, and Hope hurried to answer it.

"Hey, Hope," Kendall Vonn said as she followed Hope into the showroom carrying her guitar. Her long red hair was pulled up into a neat bun, and she was wearing an elegant red sheath dress.

"You look nice tonight," Hope said. Usually the singer was wearing a T-shirt with a long cotton skirt while she busked down by the riverfront.

"I know how to clean up when I need to." She grinned at Hope. Then she glanced around the showroom. "Where's McHottie?"

"McHottie?" Hope raised an eyebrow.

"Please." Kendall rolled her eyes. "Like you don't see how smokin' Lucas is."

"Oh, I know exactly how hot he is," Hope said, unable to keep the words from pouring out of her mouth. "We dated on and off for over ten years."

"That's right," Lucas said as he reemerged from the back, dressed in slacks and a button-down shirt. His hair was damp, and he wore that cocky grin that told Hope he'd heard every word of their conversation. "She knows all my secrets."

"Oh hell," Hope breathed and turned her back on him. This was the last thing she needed.

Adorable. His voice sounded in her head, making butterflies flutter in her gut.

Damn. Taken before I even had a shot, Kendall thought.

Hope smiled to herself, because even though she kept telling herself she wouldn't be getting back together with Lucas, there wasn't any universe where she could picture him with anyone else. And wasn't that selfish? But in that moment, she couldn't bring herself to care. She cleared her throat and pointed to the area near the front counter. "Kendall, I thought you could set up and play in that corner over there."

"I'm on it." She walked over and started setting up.

"You've done a wonderful job," Lucas said. "You have no idea how much I appreciate this."

Hope waved a hand. "Don't speak too soon. Let's see who shows up first."

"Knowing you, at least half the town will be here." He leaned over and pressed his lips to her cheek.

Hope leaned into the kiss and swallowed a sigh as her face tingled from the contact.

The bell chimed on the door, and from that moment on, the next three hours flew by as Hope reintroduced Lucas to all of the attendees as Premonition Pointe's premier furniture maker.

The place was a who's who of the coastal town. A few members of the city council, the president of the chamber of commerce, and even the mayor were all in attendance. Hope made sure to greet them all and then moved on to a group of part-time summer residents who lived in the same beachside subdivision.

"What I want to know is why no one has snatched up that glorious specimen," a tall redhead said as she took a sip of champagne.

"Someone did," Grace said, appearing from behind Gigi, who was standing quietly among her new neighbors. "But he moved to Boston, and you know how long distance goes."

Hope wanted to groan with exasperation. Yes, Lucas was a catch, but was every single woman in the town going to set her sights on him?

"So he is single then?" the redhead asked.

Grace shrugged. "He's not married, but I don't think he ever got over the one he left behind if you know what I mean."

Grace, Hope mouthed and gave her head a tiny shake.

But her friend ignored her. "I'm pretty sure he's hoping to rekindle that romance, so buyer beware if you're thinking of asking him out. Those first loves are killer. Men never seem to be able to let them go."

"Once he gets a taste of this, he won't even remember that other woman's name," the redhead said, eyeing Lucas as if he were a steak. A predatory smile claimed her lips. She turned in Lucas's direction, and then after glancing over her shoulder, she added, "Watch and learn ladies."

Hope had to stop herself from reaching out and yanking the woman back. But instead of making a complete fool of herself over the man, she slowly let out a breath, pasted a smile on her face, and said, "Excuse me. I need to introduce myself to a few more people."

But instead of mingling, Hope checked the refreshments, making sure everything was stocked, and kept her attention on the redhead who'd plastered herself to Lucas's side.

Lucas did a double take when the woman placed her hand on his chest. And Hope smiled to herself when he gently removed it and appeared to politely dismiss her as he scanned the room and met Hope's gaze. He gave her a tiny wink and then went back to talking to one of the interior designers Hope had invited.

"Looks like Lucas is definitely off the market," Grace said, appearing beside her.

"No he isn't." Hope rolled her eyes.

She chuckled. "Just keep telling yourself that." Grace squeezed her arm and added, "Owen's here. Do you mind if we take off, or do you need me to stay for moral support?"

Hope glanced over at her friend's boyfriend, who was talking to Kevin Landers, his boss. He was tanned, and his dark hair was styled in a deliberate messy windblown look. He was everything Grace's ex wasn't. Younger, sexy, attentive, and most of all, he adored and appreciated Grace. Hope had never been happier for her friend. "Go on. Have a great night."

"Love you." Grace gave her a hug and whispered, "This event was fantastic. It's going to launch Lucas's business. You know that, right?"

"That's the plan." Hope pulled back and nodded to Owen. "Now go have some fun with that man. Let me live vicariously through you."

"You don't need to live through me." Grace eyed Lucas. "Your man is right there."

Hope gave her friend a pointed look. "Go."

"All right." Grace brushed her auburn locks out of her eyes and said, "See you tomorrow for brunch?"

"Yep." Hope watched as her friend pried Owen away from Landers and couldn't help the tinge of jealousy when he wrapped his arm around her and pressed a kiss to her temple. It wasn't that she was envious that her friend had a hot younger man who adored her. She just missed that intimacy.

She glanced at Lucas again as memories of a thousand kisses slammed into her. A small ache formed in her gut, and she let out a disgusted sigh. This was not the time for memory lane. She straightened her shoulders and went back to work, mingling with the guests.

* * *

"Lucas," Hope called toward the end of the event as she waved him over. "There's someone here I'd like you to meet."

He was chatting with a pretty blonde who Hope thought might be one of the interior designers she'd invited from a couple of towns over. The designer leaned in and gave him a lingering kiss on the cheek that seemed more of an invitation than a friendly goodbye. Hope's irritation flared to life, and she had to order herself to stay put instead of physically hauling the woman away from him.

Dammit. She'd known working with Lucas was a bad idea. Here she was trying to be professional, and she'd spent the majority of the night ready to claw people's eyes out over the man. She needed to get a grip.

Lucas turned his attention to Hope, and as his gaze swept over her, that cocky half smile was back, indicating that he knew exactly what she'd been thinking.

Hope did her best to paste a neutral smile on her face and turned her attention to the tall man with the thick dark hair standing beside her. "Kyle, this is Lucas King, the owner of Against the Grain Interiors." Her gaze drifted back to Lucas. "And Lucas, this is Kyle Epps. He's the buyer for Lux and Comfort. They specialize in limited-run furniture and accessories."

"Hello." Lucas shook Kyle's hand, and the buyer immediately started praising some of Lucas's more unique pieces. He inquired about an ornate coat tree and a hand painted accent chest.

Pleased with herself, Hope moved to the front door to thank the guests for attending as they started to leave. She was in the middle of hugging Joy goodbye when she heard, *It's perfect. It's a new business in town and the ideal place to use to move the drugs. With his history with the town, no one will suspect a thing.*

Hope froze. *Move drugs?*

Everything seemed to slow down as she scanned the crowd of polished guests, trying to figure out who exactly was trying to use Lucas's shop as cover for running drugs.

Her gaze landed on the mayor and her husband, a couple realtors, Gabrielle, the town's lifestyle reporter, a few designers, and more than two dozen people she didn't recognize. And not one of them had a huge sign that said *Drug Dealer* hanging from their neck.

CHAPTER FIVE

$\mathcal{B}$y the time Hope locked the front door after the last handful of guests left the showroom, she had a pounding headache. She'd spent the last forty-five minutes straining to hear everyone's thoughts. At first when she'd tried to open her mind, she'd struggled. All she'd heard were snippets of thoughts that didn't make much sense. But as soon as she realized all she had to do was ask the universe for access, thoughts flooded in. It had been forty-five minutes of pure hell.

The thoughts were so loud and overwhelming that she'd felt as if she were standing in the middle of the room while everyone shouted at her at the same time. And putting the genie back in the bottle had proven to be near impossible. If that was what her mother felt like all the time, it was no wonder she'd run away to get some peace.

"Hope?" Lucas said from behind her.

She jumped, turning to him and placing a hand over her racing heart. It seemed impossible that she hadn't heard him coming. Not after what she'd just experienced by purposely trying to invade everyone's thoughts.

"Sorry," he said. "Didn't mean to startle you. I was just going to say that you don't need to stay. I can clean all of this up."

"What? No." She frowned and shook her head. "I'm the event planner. It's my job to clean it all up and make sure the place shines before I leave."

"You've already outdone yourself." He gave her an appreciative smile. "The caliber of clients you attracted is going to jumpstart my business here in a major way. I've already made appointments to work out details with over a dozen people next week. Damn, Hope, it's already clear I'm woefully underpaying you for the service you provide. In fact, I think I'm going to give you a commission for every client you brought me with this event."

Hope felt her cheeks flush with pride, and she couldn't help but grin at him. He really was the best guy she'd ever known. "No way. I was just doing my job."

He let out a laugh and shook his head. "No, Hope. I hired you to organize an open house. You did that and then went above and beyond by acting as my publicist. What you did here tonight was incredible. Thank you."

She took a step forward and pressed her hand to his chest right over his heart. "You're welcome." Then she took a step back and added, "I just did what I'd do for anyone."

He raised one skeptical eyebrow. "Really?"

A chuckle escaped from the back of her throat. "No. Your event might have gotten a little extra attention."

"And why's that exactly?" There was a challenge in his expression that told her he knew why, but she'd be damned if she'd give him the satisfaction by admitting that she'd done it because she desperately wanted his business to be a success.

"I'm trying to build my own business. By inviting a bunch of businesspeople from town, they'll remember me when they need an event organizer."

He pursed his lips and nodded. "And the fact that you're the only event organizer in town isn't enough?"

"Nope. I've got competition from three surrounding towns. And Peggy Pitsman just hung her shingle a few months ago. Mostly she's doing baby showers, but I heard she put on a luncheon for the book club recently. I need to stay on top of my game."

"I see." His lips twitched, and his eyes crinkled as he held back a laugh.

She rolled her eyes as if she were irritated with him, but the truth was she missed bantering with him and couldn't deny that this felt good. But there were more important things to talk about than why she'd put so much effort into his event. She cleared her throat. "Listen, there's something I need to talk to you about."

A flicker of concern flashed in his silver gaze, but it disappeared just as quickly. "Sure. Why don't we sit." He led her to a dining room table that was on display and pulled out one of the chairs for her.

She took her seat and waited for him to sit in the chair to her left. Hope clasped her hands together and turned to him, looking into his eyes. "Remember when I told you that my mom is back in town?"

"Sure." He furrowed his brow. "How are you doing with that? Are you okay?"

Lucas knew better than anyone her issues with her mom.

39

"Honestly, I don't really know." She glanced down at the table, studying the varying shades of color in the hardwood. "Something happened last night."

He placed a hand over hers and squeezed, not saying a word.

A small smile tugged at her lips, and some of the weight on her chest lifted. He knew her so well. If he just waited her out, she'd tell him everything. Probably more than if he asked questions. When there was something important on her mind, her way of dealing with it was to think it through while talking. If he asked questions, she was more likely to clam up. "I was at the cliffs with Grace and Joy, and I heard their thoughts."

"You just heard their thoughts? Like Grace was thinking about her next curse on her ex while Joy was contemplating which sex toys she's going to order next?" His eyes danced with humor.

Hope cackled. "How did you know about the sex toys?"

"Joy told me. I ran into her at the café, and she kinda asked me for advice." He chuckled.

"No effing way," Hope gasped out and then covered her mouth as she started laughing again. She laughed so hard tears started streaming down her face. "Please tell me she'd been drinking."

"You know, I thought that at first. I even asked her if she'd spiked her coffee, but I think she just needed a guy's perspective about Paul's indifference." He shrugged. "I'm not sure I helped, though."

Hope leaned in. "What did you tell her?"

"That a man is usually not subtle when he's interested and that she should probably just have an honest conversation with him about what she needs."

"That is not a conversation I'd want to have with Paul. Can you even imagine? I bet he uses terms like 'privates' and 'special parts.'"

"He's definitely uptight," Lucas said, chuckling. Then he sobered as he scanned his gaze over Hope.

The air turned thick between them, and Hope had a moment where she was certain he wanted to kiss her. Everything inside of her yearned to lean forward, to feel his lips on hers once more. But instead of letting herself fall right back into old habits, she glanced away and said, "When I got home last night after spending time with Grace and Joy, my mom told me that the women in my family are cursed with telepathy when we turn forty-six. It was why she left. She said she couldn't control it, and that she left for both of us. So I'd have my privacy and so that she didn't lose her mind."

Lucas blinked. "Telepathy? Seriously?"

She nodded. "Seriously."

"That's... wow. She was reading your mind? Way back when you were a teenager?"

"Yep." She watched him as he eventually came to the same realization that she had.

His face flushed, and he looked so very much like the nervous teenager she'd once fallen in love with. It made her heart ache with nostalgia. "That was when we... uh, were doing all kinds of things I prayed your mom would never know about."

"Exactly." She threw her head back and laughed. "Can you even imagine having a teenager and having to read their thoughts?"

"No. Not at all." He shook his head, looking horrified. Then after a minute, he narrowed his eyes at her and asked,

"You said the women in your family are cursed with telepathy at forty-six. Does that mean you've been reading my mind all night?"

"No. I only got a couple of snippets of thoughts. Like when you thought I was adorable."

"You *are* adorable. Sexy and smart, too, just in case you missed those." He winked at her, and she smiled back, unable to resist the spell he was casting over her. "Do you know what I'm thinking right now?"

She stared him in the eye and concentrated. A vision of the two of them walking hand in hand down at Premonition Beach flashed in her mind. Tears stung her eyes, and she had to blink them back. That had been one of their things that they did when they just wanted to spend time together. The memories of all the time they'd spent down there in what they'd always called 'their cove' were too much. She couldn't go there right then. Not without breaking down. So instead of confirming his thoughts of the beach, she said, "You're thinking about the time we broke into Grayson Masterson's rental and spent the night drinking in his hot tub."

He eyed her skeptically, but then he flashed her his sexy half smile that showed off his dimple. "No, but I am now. Remember what happened after we got out of the hot tub? I seem to recall a midnight swim in the ocean followed by—"

"Stop!" She laughed. "No need to voice that memory. I think it's one neither of us will forget."

"Fair enough. But what do you say to a repeat? I'm pretty sure I can still pick the lock on Grayson's gate. I wouldn't mind a soak in that hot tub."

She grinned at him. "As tempting as that sounds, I'm pretty sure Grayson has security cameras now. I'd rather not put myself in a position where my goods end up on video."

"Damn. Too bad. I was just starting to get excited about the idea." He leaned back in his chair and grinned back at her.

To be honest, so had she. But there was no way she was going to admit that. Besides, they had something a lot more important to discuss. "Listen, there's something else I need to tell you."

His smile vanished, and his expression turned serious. "Okay. What's wrong?"

She glanced down at her hands, noticing that she'd unknowingly balled them into fists. Hope flattened her hands out on the table and looked back up at him. "I heard someone thinking that your business would be the perfect place to use to run drugs. It sounded like they were scoping you and your place out."

Lucas's frown deepened. "Drugs? That's... not possible. You know I'm not involved with anything to do with drugs. Hell, it's been over twenty years since I even lit up a joint."

"I didn't say you were involved. I said they wanted to use your store, and I wanted to tell you so you'd know someone you'd met tonight doesn't have your best interests at heart."

He made a face and waved a hand dismissing her concerns. "You know I'd never get involved in anything like that. And no one is going to be able to move drugs through my shop without me being in on it, right?"

"I guess so. I just feel terrible for inviting someone like that here."

"Hope," he said gently. "You put out a press release, just as you should. You can't help who showed up. Do you have any idea who it was?"

She shook her head. "No, but I'm going to keep an ear out and see if I can figure it out before they become a problem.

You know, since I can hear thoughts now, I should be able to find something out."

"And then do what with that information?" he asked, narrowing his eyes.

"I don't know. Alert the Premonition Pointe police? Let you know so you don't end up in business with them? That kind of thing."

"That's a noble thing to do," he said. "But, Hope, I think it's best if you don't go looking for trouble. I really just don't want you to end up in some drug kingpin's crosshairs."

"I'm not looking for trouble. I'm just—"

"You're not?" He chuckled and shook his head. "Getting in the way of drug dealers is the definition of trouble." He stood and held out his hand to her.

She sighed, hating both that he was telling her what to do and that he was right. What did she know about drug dealers other than what she'd seen on television? Hope took his hand and let him help her up.

"Want to go for a cup of coffee or... a walk on the beach maybe?" he asked.

She gave him a soft smile. "I would love to do both, but I don't think so."

He pulled her closer to him and stared down at her. "Why not?"

"You know why." She pushed up on her tiptoes, gave him a light kiss on the cheek, and then patted his chest. "Now, I'm going to take you up on that offer to finish cleaning up, and I'm going to take off."

"All right," he said softly and pulled her in, giving her a tight hug.

She held on with everything she had for a few seconds,

and then she pulled away and walked out without looking back.

CHAPTER SIX

"More coffee?" Hope asked Grace and Joy as she rose from the table in Pointe of View Café.

Joy groaned and shook her head. "Better make mine decaf."

"Decaf? Seriously?" Grace asked her, looking like someone had just suggested she throw out her favorite designer heels. "Since when do you drink decaf?"

"Since too much caffeine started making my boobs hurt." She pressed her hands to her chest and grimaced. "I can have one cup, but any more than that and they just ache. My doctor told me this sometimes happens when you get older."

Hope blinked at her. Caffeine was like her life's blood and the only thing that got her through some days. "You're kidding right? Please tell me you're messing with us."

"I wish I was." Joy lowered her hands and pressed them against the table. "Getting older sucks donkey shlong."

"Jeez, Joy. I'm so sorry," Grace said then looked up at Hope. "Get me another. Large. I'll drink Joy's share."

"Gee thanks." Joy rolled her eyes.

Hope made her way up to the bar, order two more coffees from Jackson, the recent college grad who was working as a barista while trying to figure out his next move, and then retreated back to the table. After handing the coffee to Grace, Hope made a face and dug into her oversized cinnamon roll.

"Hey, just be glad you're not suffering tendonitis in your right hip and ankle," Grace said dramatically. "The other night when Owen and I were in bed—"

"That's quite enough." Joy held her hand up, stopping her friend. "I do not want to hear about your sexual escapades right now. It's too depressing. I can't even get Paul to give me a back rub these days. I swear, if I didn't know better, I'd think the man was having an affair."

Grace and Hope shared a look.

"Stop," Joy said with a sigh. "I know what you're thinking, but I really don't think that's it. He's just… not into it for some reason."

"You really don't think it's because he's into it with someone else?" Hope asked gently.

"No. He works a lot, but he comes home exhausted and frustrated with work. There's a lot of tension. I just really don't think it's an affair. Besides, he's terrified of STDs. And if someone was willing to have an affair with a married man, he'd never trust them." She shrugged. "I keep asking him to go to therapy, but he refuses."

"I'm sorry, honey," Grace said, squeezing Joy's hand. Grace had recently been through her own divorce, but in her case, her husband had been sticking it to the office receptionist. There hadn't been a relationship to work on after he'd walked in one day and said it was over and he was marrying his side piece. "We're here if you want to talk about it."

"She's right. And I won't even tell you to dump his sorry ass, even if it is what I'm thinking," Hope said, giving her friend a sympathetic smile, wanting to make sure she knew that, no matter what, she was on Joy's side.

Joy's clear blue eyes clouded with tears, but she blinked them back and nodded. "I know. I love you both, but right now I'd rather talk about literally anything other than Paul. I'm just so sick of whining about my relationship."

"It's not whining. If you can't talk to us, who can you talk to?" Hope asked.

"Ditto," Grace added.

"Thanks." Joy sniffed. "Now, make me feel better by telling me I'm not the only one with weird perimenopause symptoms.

They both laughed.

"I had inch long face hairs that seem to pop up overnight," Grace said. "And my hair is starting to turn gray."

"Your dye job is doing a great job of covering that up," Hope said.

"Not that hair." Grace glanced down at her crotch and raised one eyebrow. "Things are definitely changing colors."

"Oh." Joy placed a hand over her mouth, unable to control her giggles. "I, um, haven't had that issue just yet."

"That's because you're a blonde," Hope said, laughing with her. This was what she loved most in her life. The time she spent with her girlfriends filled her soul. Who needed ex-boyfriends when she had this in her life?

"Grace?" a man called from a few tables away.

Hope turned and spotted a tall handsome man with silver

hair and green eyes holding a cup of coffee. Matt something. He was the man who'd purchased one of the haunted houses Grace sold earlier in the year. And damn, was he sexy. She couldn't help imagining what it would be like to skinny dip in his hot tub. Lucas immediately popped into her mind, making guilt wash over her, and she wanted to scream. She had nothing to feel guilty about. Lucas was not her boyfriend.

Not now. But how long until he is? she asked herself.

She gritted her teeth against the thought and put Lucas out of her mind. Nothing good would come from considering getting back together with him.

"Matt!" Grace jumped out of her seat and rushed over to him, giving him a quick hug. "It's been a while since I've seen you. What have you been up to?"

"Oh, you know. Spending time at the beach with my kids and their families. But they've left now and it's just me. I've been working remotely. Can't beat sitting on the deck during conference calls, right?"

"Sounds fabulous." She turned back to the table. "Joy, Hope, you remember Matt Dahl, right?"

"Sure," Joy said.

"Who could forget Matt?" Hope said, smiling at him. "He's the most eligible bachelor in town."

He chuckled. "Grace didn't think so."

Grace's face turned pink as she flushed. "Hey now. I was and still am dating someone else."

"My loss." Matt turned his attention back to Hope and eyed her. *Now that's who I should've asked out. All those gorgeous black curls would look fantastic splayed over my pillow.*

Hope was momentarily speechless. Holy shit. Was this her life now? Hearing Matt's unguarded thoughts was unsettling. What would he have done if he'd heard her first thoughts about him? Drag her off to his beach house? There was a reason people didn't just blurt out every thought they had. It wasn't civilized.

"Did you want to join us?" Grace asked.

Hope shot her a glare, but she was too busy focusing on Matt to notice.

"Sure." He took the empty seat next to Hope and placed his coffee cup on the table. "How've you been, Hope?"

"Good." She took a sip of her coffee and stared out the window at the incredible view.

"I heard the open house at Against the Grain was a huge hit," he added. "It's all anyone is talking about this morning."

She turned to stare at him. "It is?"

"Sure. A couple members of the bird watcher's club were out front talking about it, and earlier when I stopped at the post office, the lady in front of me was raving about the new woodworker in town."

Hope snorted. She just bet she was. "The bird watcher's club? None of those ladies were there last night."

"They were reading the glowing writeup about it in the *Premonition Perspective*."

That was the gossip rag in town that came out once a week. "At least it was positive."

"Oh, our bestie is the talk of the town," Grace said. "Hope, I bet your voicemail is going to be overflowing with new clients later today."

"We'll see," Hope said, brushing off the prediction. She was still certain that most everyone was just wagging their tongues about Lucas moving back to town.

"I hope you're not too busy for dinner," Matt said, giving her a sexy half smile.

A vision of Matt pressing her up against the wall and

devouring her mouth flashed in her mind, and for the life of her, she had no idea if that was her thought or his. "I—"

"Of course she does," Joy said. "In fact, she's been dying to go to that new place on Ocean. Abalone? Right, Hope?"

"Right." Hope shook her head, already knowing there was no backing out of this without looking like a complete jackass.

"So have I," Matt said, grinning at her. "What do you say, Hope? Are you free for dinner Friday night? I could get us reservations at Abalone and then we could take a drive up the coast to watch the sunset."

"Yes," Grace and Joy said at the same time.

Hope rolled her eyes. "I think my social directors have spoken."

Matt nodded. "Yeah, I heard them. But I'm a lot more interested in your answer."

The playfulness was gone, and his sincerity touched her. How could she say no to that? He was sexy and fun and not Lucas. "Yes. I'd love to."

The scene of him pressing her up against the wall flashed in her mind again just as something that looked a lot like desire flashed in his eyes. Then he said, "I'm looking forward to it."

"Me, too." But as soon as she said the words, she knew it was a lie. All she felt was anxiety.

He handed her his phone. "Mind putting your info in there? I'll call you to confirm the time."

She did as he asked, and a moment later he was saying his goodbyes and walking away. After the café door closed behind him, she turned on her friends. "What is wrong with you two?"

"What?" Grace asked, but Joy at least had the decency to look ashamed of herself.

"You guys left me no way of backing out of that gracefully. Now I have to have dinner with him on Friday, and then I have a date with Benji on Saturday."

"And you're complaining, why?" Joy asked with both eyebrows raised. *She has no idea what I'd do for a date with just one hot guy, much less two.*

Hope sighed. How could she sit there and complain about a robust dating life when one of her besties was having such a hard time getting her husband to pay attention to her. She forced a smile and said, "Not complaining. Just a little surprised. It's been a while since I've juggled dating two men."

Grace placed her fist to her mouth and pretended to cough as she said, "Three."

"Not three," Hope insisted. "Just Matt and Benji. Lucas doesn't stand a chance."

"Sure. If you say so," Grace said, winking at her. "But we'll see."

CHAPTER SEVEN

"*I*'m out," Grace said. "I have a house showing in ten." She got up and held her arms out, waiting for her hug.

Hope reluctantly got to her feet, still annoyed at her friend. Grace was in a happy relationship, with a younger guy no less. She wasn't having any problems in the bedroom department. If Joy hadn't been there, Hope would've let her have it for pushing her into a date with Matt. She leaned in, gave Grace a hug, and said, "We'll be discussing this later. You know that, right?"

Grace chuckled and whispered back, "I had no doubt. Just go easy on Joy."

"Yep."

Hope sat back down and watched as Joy hugged Grace goodbye.

When it was just the two of them, Joy looked over at Hope. "I'm sorry. I know that was over the line."

"Don't worry about it. I guess it won't kill me to have dinner with a silver fox." Hope waved a hand, dismissing

Joy's apology. Even if she was fairly certain all Matt wanted to do was rip her clothes off. It wasn't lost on her that, before Lucas had returned, she would've been perfectly fine with that. Now she didn't know what she thought. She just knew she wasn't likely to fall into bed with a stranger. It didn't feel right.

Joy gave her a grateful smile. "I know I was out of line. Thanks for letting me off the hook."

Hope was about to once again absolve her from her sin, but before she could get any words out, someone shouted, "Hey! Watch out!"

Jackson flew out from behind the counter and lunged for a tall, lean young man in ripped jeans and a tight black T-shirt. But before he got to the customer, the man stumbled backward right into a fancy display of ceramic mugs.

Hope and Joy both stood and raised their hands, each of them shouting, "Levitate!"

There was nothing they could do for the customer. He was already in motion and took the display down with him, along with a handful of mugs, but the majority were saved by the spell and floated in the air.

"Back up," Hope ordered all the customers surrounding the man splayed out on the floor. "Give him some air!"

Jackson waved the customers back. "Give Hope and Joy space to put the mugs down."

The customers retreated, and Joy was able to guide all the mugs to the ground without breaking any more.

Hope ran over to where Jackson was standing over the customer, shaking his head. "What happened?" she asked.

"He ordered a coffee cake, and then before he could get his drink order out, he started shaking violently and stumbled backward right into the display," Jackson said.

Kneeling, Hope placed a hand on the man's chest. His heart was racing, and his eyes were shifting back and forth in a rapid motion. "I think he's having a seizure. Someone call an ambulance."

"I'm on it," Joy said, already tapping on her phone.

Hope turned her attention back to the man and pressed two fingers to his wrist. Yes, his heart rate was definitely too elevated. And his skin was clammy to the touch. She didn't have any idea what to do in this situation. All she knew was that the man wasn't in good shape, and she was going to stay by his side until the paramedics arrived.

She didn't have to wait long. The sirens sounded in the distance, and even though it seemed like hours went by, Hope was certain the two women who rushed into the café in uniform had come as fast as they could.

"I've got it from here," the woman with bronze skin said, gently nudging Hope aside. Her partner, a tall dark-haired woman with her jaw set, took her place on the other side of the man and immediately went to work administering an IV.

"Looks like a drug overdose." The bronze-skinned woman looked up. "Anyone know what he took?"

Everyone, including Jackson, was silent.

"Anyone know this man?" she asked.

"His name is Spencer," Jackson said. "He comes in here a couple times a week. I think he works over at Cryptic."

Cryptic was the local bookstore down on Main that also had a huge section of board games and puzzles.

"All right." She sighed and told her partner they needed to get him to emergency ASAP for a tox screen. The two paramedics were fast and efficient, getting the man on the gurney and expertly wheeling him out to their vehicle.

Jackson stared at them through the front window and ran a hand through his dark curly hair.

"Are you all right?" Hope asked him, lightly squeezing his arm.

He shook his head. "That's the third OD this town has had in two weeks. The second one I've personally witnessed." He glanced down at her, his eyes full of worry, and she noticed his hands were shaking slightly. "Before I left for college four years ago, I knew there were some people in town who did drugs, but they were a small population that usually just kept to themselves out on their land where no one would know what they were up to. But wow, have things changed. First there was Lex's Mom's boyfriend and that crowd he was hanging out with, and now this guy, a nineteen-year-old girl, and a woman in her thirties. I don't know what's happening or why our town is suddenly a hotbed for drug use, but it's really got me shaken."

Hope placed a hand on his arm for reassurance, but then pulled him into a hug. "You did great handling this."

He let out a scoff. "No. You did. You're the one who kept him from falling into a pile of broken cups, and you sat with him until the paramedics got here."

"You kept the customers calm and didn't freak out. You did good. Trust me. Now come sit down with me and Joy for a minute." She started to tug him toward their table.

"I can't. I have to clean up this mess and get back behind the counter."

Hope glanced over to see one of the staffers had already righted the display and was busy sweeping up the broken shards, while a young woman had stepped behind the counter to take care of the few customers who'd stuck around. "I think your coworkers have it under control."

Jackson followed her gaze and then slowly nodded. "Yeah. Okay. But just a minute. I want to make sure they are okay, too."

Once Hope got him seated, Joy passed him a bottle of water she'd retrieved while they'd been talking.

"Drink this," she said.

He grabbed the bottle but didn't lift it to his lips. "Do you think he'll be all right?"

"I hope so," Hope said, remembering what she'd heard the night before at Lucas's opening about someone wanting to use his shop to move drugs. She wondered if that person was already distributing drugs and if he or she was the one responsible for the overdoses. A chill ran up her spine. Premonition Pointe had always been a relatively safe beach town. If drugs were taking over, she didn't see how she had a choice other than to try to find out who was at the center of it. "How well do you know him?"

"Not well at all." Jackson finally took a drink of the water. "He's a customer who's flirted with me a few times. I'd actually been trying to work up the nerve to ask him out, but the last few times he came in, it was clear he was on something, so I abandoned that idea. I don't need that shit in my life, you know?"

Hope nodded.

"Then this happened today, and I don't know how I feel. Shocked, I guess. Worried. Pissed that drugs have found their way here. You know I was hoping to build my graphic arts business here and just settle down with a cute guy and a couple of dogs and enjoy life. But now I'm wondering if I made a mistake."

"You didn't," Joy said, shaking her head. "This town is too

resilient to let drugs take over, right, Hope?" her friend asked, sounding as if she needed Hope to reassure her.

What if that had been one of my kids? Joy's thoughts were as clear as day. Hope gave her a reassuring smile. "Of course it is. And I have some ideas on what we can do to help."

"You do?" Jackson and Joy asked at the same time.

"Yep." She quickly filled Jackson in on her new telepathic ability.

His eyes went wide, and his mouth fell open before he cleared his throat and asked, "You're a mind reader now?"

"Not exactly. I sometimes hear random thoughts. But I haven't heard any from you."

He let out a nervous chuckle. "Does that mean I'm simple minded?" Jackson tapped his temple. "Nothing going on up here?"

"If that's the case, then so is everyone else. I don't hear a lot. Just snippets here and there. For instance, I heard Joy worrying about her children getting caught up in the drugs, but that's all."

"It terrifies me that one of them will fall into the wrong crowd, make some dumb decision, and then the next thing you know, something like this happens." She waved a hand toward the display. "We've all heard the stories. Sometimes all it takes is once to get addicted."

Hope nodded. "Yes, that worries me, too. For your kids, for Lex, for you, Jackson."

Jackson jerked back. "I wouldn't do drugs. That's not my thing."

She believed him, but he was also a twenty-two-year-old who'd just graduated from college and was living in a small town while trying to make it on his own. "I know, but it doesn't stop me from worrying. You've been friends with

Lex and Kyle for so long I feel like your auntie. The worry comes with the territory."

He rolled his eyes, but she didn't miss the tiny twitch of a smile that he hid. He was a good kid; she knew that. She just wanted to keep him and the rest of the young people of the town safe. Not to mention that she didn't want Lucas's business anywhere near drug runners. If they decided to use him and his business, who knew what they'd do to try to force him into it? Those types of people didn't play nice.

"So, now that you know I have this new superpower," she said. "I can tell you that last night when I was at Lucas's open house at Against the Grain, I heard someone thinking that his business would be a perfect place to use to run drugs."

"What? You don't think he'd do something like that do you," Joy asked.

"No, he wouldn't. At least not the Lucas that I know," Hope agreed.

"Who was thinking that?" Jackson asked.

She shrugged. "I don't know. The place was crowded, and I couldn't connect the thoughts to a specific person. I don't even know what they meant by 'run drugs through his business.' He sells handmade furniture and accessories. Unless they are smuggling drugs in through his wood shipments, it doesn't make any sense to me. And even if they were doing that, they'd need Lucas's cooperation to get their goods."

Jackson and Joy were silent as they gave each other a skeptical look.

"What?" Hope asked.

"You can't tell what we're thinking?" Jackson asked, his eyes narrowed.

"No, but if you're asking me to try to read your mind, I

can do that. It's not something I particularly *want* to be able to do, but I'll work it if I have to."

Joy sighed. "I think we're both wondering just how much we can trust Lucas. He's been gone for a long time, and now he's back with what looks like a pretty good-sized bank account. He bought a house with a fair amount of property and then turned around and opened a retail business. Both of those presumably take a fair bit of capital."

Hope gritted her teeth and tried not to lash out at her friend for suggesting that Lucas might have any part in the drug trade. She *knew* him. Knew in her bones that he wouldn't ever be a part of such an operation. "*I* trust him. That's all we need to know."

Neither of them said anything, and suddenly there was tension in the air.

Hope sat back with her arms crossed over her chest. "I'd know, all right?"

"Because you're telepathic now?" Jackson asked.

"No. Because I'd know and that's all there is to it." She knew she sounded rigid and like she couldn't face the truth about someone she loved. But her gut was telling her she wasn't wrong, and she was a woman who always followed her gut.

"All right. Trust me, I definitely want to believe Lucas wouldn't be involved in something like this," Joy said gently. "And that's what we'll do unless there's some reason to believe otherwise."

"There won't be," Hope insisted.

"You're right, Hope," Jackson said. "I think we're all just a little flustered. Let's focus on who might be behind the drugs. Any ideas?"

"Can you find out the names of the three people who overdosed?" Hope asked him.

"Yeah, I think so. I can certainly shake the gossip tree."

"Perfect. Just keep it quiet. I don't want anyone to find out you're asking questions. We just don't know how dangerous these people are."

Jackson nodded. "No problem. My gay network knows how to keep stuff on the downlow."

Hope chuckled. "Understood."

"What can I do?" Joy asked.

"You're going to be my partner in crime while we check out everyone who showed up at Lucas's open house last night," Hope said. "You'll be the one looking for services, and I'll be your sidekick. We'll find a way to bring up the issue, and I'll try to listen in on their thoughts. We'll also get Grace to investigate who is new in town. See if there's a connection."

"Definitely. I'm up for it," Joy said, sitting up straighter. "Let's take out the trash." She put her fist up, waiting for a three-way fist bump.

Hope met her halfway, and then the pair of them stared at Jackson, waiting for him to join them in their show of solidarity.

Jackson groaned and made a face as he reluctantly put his fist out. "This is so uncool."

"Maybe, but you love us anyway," Hope said. Then she stood and pulled him out of his chair and gave him a big hug.

CHAPTER EIGHT

"*H*ope?" Angela Anderson called as she walked through Hope's house. "Are you still here?"

Hope leaned against the counter and thought, *Can't you hear me?*

"Yes, I can now." Angela rounded the corner and narrowed her eyes at her daughter. "Seriously? Is this how it's going to be now?"

A flash of guilt swept through Hope. Why was her default with her mother always so combative? "Sorry. You didn't deserve that."

Angela sighed. "I know we still have issues to work out, and I don't expect us to work out everything overnight. I just hoped that we could start trying."

"Yeah, okay. But Grace and Joy are on their way over to start working on a project. Now isn't really a great time." Hope pulled a mug out of the cabinet and poured herself a cup of coffee, wondering if it was too early in the day to add Irish whiskey.

"It's five o'clock somewhere," Angela said, giving her a cheeky smile.

Hope forced herself to keep her expression neutral instead of rolling her eyes like a teenager. Her mother had already told her she couldn't really control what she heard, so Hope shouldn't be surprised. What was interesting was that Hope didn't hear things so clearly. She got snippets, and sometimes if she tried, she'd get a little more, but she definitely wasn't being bombarded with thoughts all the time the way her mother described her own experience. Even though she knew her mother had probably heard everything she was thinking, she went ahead and verbalized her thoughts. "Is this curse going to get worse as time goes on? Am I suddenly going to wake up one day and start hearing *everything* everyone thinks?"

"I don't know, Hope," she said with a shrug. "For me, it was overwhelming right from the start. For your grandmother, too. If you're lucky, maybe your curse won't be as overwhelming."

"If I'm lucky," Hope agreed.

"I just wanted to let you know I'm heading out for the rest of the day. I'll be back for dinner. Do you want me to cook something?"

Hope shook her head. "No thanks. I'm going out with the girls."

Her mother eyed her with suspicion. Hope just raised her chin slightly, silently daring her to question the statement. "Okay. Text me if anything changes."

"It probably won't," Hope said and tried to ignore the pangs of regret. She'd always envied Joy's relationship with her mother. They were tight. The best of friends. It was something she'd wanted, especially considering she didn't have any other close family. Instead, she'd ended up making Grace and Joy her family. It worked for her, but that didn't mean she didn't feel the loss, nonetheless.

Angela nodded as she left the kitchen. A moment later, Hope heard the front door close softly as her mother left to do whatever she was going to do. Hope hadn't even bothered to ask. Who did that?

Hope flopped down into a chair at her dining room table and buried her head in her hands. She was the worst daughter ever. First, she'd been rude, not once, but twice. And then, she'd lied about her dinner plans knowing her mother would see right through her.

She groaned and mentally berated herself for how she was handling her mother's visit. If she kept being so childish, she was going to have to see a therapist about her mommy issues. She'd end up hating herself if she couldn't find a way to meet her mother in the middle.

Hope got up from the table and moved into the kitchen. Without even thinking about it, she started pulling flour, sugar, and chocolate chips from her cupboard.

Forty-five minutes later, as she was pulling the cookies out of the oven, there was a loud knock on her door, followed by Grace calling out, "We're here! Oh, son of a chocolate fairy. Do I smell cookies?"

"Yep. I'm in the kitchen." Hope pulled two mugs out of her cabinet and set them on the counter.

Grace appeared first, wearing a chic white suit. Her auburn hair was tied into a sophisticated twist, and she looked like a million bucks. Joy followed her, and Hope did a double take when she saw her. Joy was the one who was always put together, but shockingly, she was wearing yoga pants and a gray T-shirt that said *Not Today, Satan* on the front. Her long blond hair was tied into a messy braid on one side, and her eyes were red as if she'd been crying.

"What happened?" Hope asked, automatically handing Joy a cookie.

Joy popped the entire cookie into her mouth and collapsed into one of the chairs at the table.

"It's that bad?" Hope went to the kitchen and poured each of them a cup of coffee.

Joy nodded and mumbled something around the cookie.

"I think that means yes," Grace said, grabbing the plate of cookies.

Considering Joy's state, Hope grabbed the bottle of Irish whiskey and put it on the tray with the coffee mugs.

Once they were all seated, Hope passed Grace her mug and then slid one to Joy and said, "Decaf just for you."

Grace grabbed the Irish whiskey, and without even asking, she poured a dollop into each of their cups.

"I'm glad someone else did it so I didn't have to feel guilty about day drinking," Hope said, giving Grace a high five. Then she turned her attention to Joy. "What's up, sweetie? Is everything okay with the kids?"

Joy nodded and took a gulp of her coffee. "Kids are fine. Hunter is going to lose his shit on his dad when he finds out, but they'll survive."

"Did he have an affair?" Grace asked tentatively.

"No. I don't think so. In fact, I'm pretty sure the man has forgotten how to use his dick."

Hope couldn't help it; she let out a startled bark of laughter. "Surely that's not something someone just forgets, is it?"

"Paul seems to have mastered it." Joy's tone was bitter and full of finality.

"Are you sure he doesn't need some help in the form of a little blue pill?" Grace asked.

They'd had the erectile dysfunction discussion before, and Joy insisted that wasn't the issue.

"Oh, no. It works. I've seen the evidence every morning for as long as I can remember. Except instead of letting me help him with it, he prefers to jerk it in the shower. He's always said he's not able to deal with anything until his morning coffee. Can you believe that? What man doesn't want a freakin' blow job first thing in the morning?"

Hope cringed. She'd known Joy and Paul had been having trouble in the bedroom for a while now, but she supposed she hadn't realized just *how* bad it had gotten.

"Okay, so you've finally had enough?" Grace asked. "Did you throw him out?"

Joy scoffed. "Who me? Throw him out over sex? No. Just two nights ago we had the big sex talk. You know, the one about how we need to find a way to connect. That we have to try. That *he* has to try. That I can't be the only one who cares about reviving our sex life. I thought it went pretty well. We'd scheduled a date for last night, just the two of us. No pressure. Just a night to shower together. Maybe a massage. Some cuddling. And then we'd see where things went. But do you know what I got instead?"

Hope was almost afraid to ask. "Don't tell me he got you a dildo."

A look of pure irritation flashed through Joy's bloodshot eyes. "You know, I think I would've appreciated that gesture. At least it would've communicated that he cared about my needs. But no. I didn't even get that much. Instead, he told me I was demanding too much. That I was oversexed, unreasonable, and that he was just done."

"Done? What does that mean?" Hope asked, wanting to jump up from the table and run down to Paul's accounting firm so she could bitch-slap him for the way he'd treated Joy. She deserved the world, and the fact that the man hadn't even come close to giving it to her just pissed Hope right off.

"He's moving out. Says he wants a trial separation, and he's already rented a small beach house on the other side of town. Which means he's known about this for at least a week, even before our big talk. Even though he thinks I don't pay attention to the finances, I noticed a four-figure withdrawal. I didn't ask him about it because I thought maybe he was trying to surprise me with a gift. You know, jewelry or a trip or something. The man just doesn't spend money unless it's on something special. Now I know it was first, last, and a deposit on a house. There's no surprise coming other than the fact that I don't have to listen to his snoring for the time being."

"He wants a trial separation, but he went ahead and signed a lease? For how long?" Grace asked.

"He said the lease was for six months." Joy grabbed her coffee and took another long gulp. "But that's a lie. I called and found out the lease is for a year. Paul is done. Grace, I think I need the number of your divorce lawyer."

"Sure, honey." Grace draped an arm around her friend and gave Hope a what-the-hell look.

"He just dumped this on you today? All because you wanted to work on your sex life?" Hope asked, trying to understand.

"Yeah. I guess." Joy sniffled. But when she looked up her face was set with determination. "You know what? I've tried everything. Been the most patient wife known to man. And if he doesn't appreciate me, then all I can say is good. I don't need to waste any more time on that asshat. I'm going to be like you two. Sign me up for a younger man or casual sex, or hell, even just someone who doesn't go to bed at nine o'clock. I'm smart. I can get a job and find someone who doesn't think I'm past my prime." She pulled her phone out of her pocket and started tapping on the screen. "What do I need to do, sign up for Tinder? Or is there another hookup app out there I don't know about?"

Hope let out a choke of laughter and took the phone from her friend. "Okay, slow down just a touch."

"Why? Do you know how long it's been since I've had an orgasm with someone else in the room?" Joy asked.

"Uh…" Hope grabbed a cookie and stuffed it in her mouth, exceedingly grateful that her telepathy seemed to be on the fritz at the moment. The last thing she wanted was a visual of whatever was going on in Joy's mind.

"I think what Hope meant was that maybe you should give yourself a bit of time before you jump back into the man pool. You know, settle just a little. Make sure you know what it is you're looking for before—"

"Orgasms, Grace. Orrrrgasms. You know, the thing you get on the regular with Owen?" Joy insisted. "That's all I want or need from a man. And the sooner the better."

"All right then." Hope grabbed Joy's phone and got busy downloading the Tinder app. One she had it open, she quickly made Joy an account. "Got a picture you want to use?"

Joy blinked at her. "You want me to put my picture on the internet? On a profile in an app that is specifically for hooking up? Are you crazy?"

"It's not just an app for hooking up, Joy," Grace said, rubbing her temple as if she were getting a headache. "People do meet on there and actually start dating. You know that, right?"

"Yeah, whatever. But that's not what I'm looking for. Not after over twenty years of Paul and his damned schedules." She turned to Hope. "Make sure you put I'm not looking for anything serious."

Hope chuckled. "I'm not putting that in there. You'll end up with every random horndog from here to San Diego messaging you. How about we just put in a few of your interests and go from there."

Joy rolled her eyes. "Fine. But I'm still not putting my picture up."

"You already did." Hope grinned at her.

"What?" Joy grabbed the phone out of Hope's hand and started scrolling through her profile. When she saw the picture, she looked up and smiled. "That one actually makes me look pretty."

"It makes you look sexy." Hope took the phone back and showed the picture of Joy to Grace. It was a profile of Joy on the beach in a bikini with a wraparound skirt and her blond hair blowing in the breeze as if she were in a shampoo commercial. It had been taken a few years ago, but Joy hadn't changed one bit. Hope handed the phone back to Joy and said, "You'll have your pick of the local hotties soon enough."

"That's good." Joy nodded but started to look unsure. "It's good to move on, right?"

"Of course it is." Grace reached over and squeezed her hand. "Just maybe don't put any pressure on yourself."

"Grace is right," Hope said. "It's fine to try to start a new chapter. We just want you to take care of yourself and do whatever is going to make you happy. If going out on a date is what you need, go do it. Have fun. You deserve some fun.

But you might want to give it some time before you dive into anything."

"You mean four hours isn't enough?" Joy asked, letting out a half laugh, half sob.

Hope and Grace both got up and wrapped their arms around Joy and held her as she cried.

It wasn't long before Joy gently brushed them off and wiped at her eyes. "I'm okay. Thank you. I just... He blindsided me, you know?"

"We know," Grace said, handing her a tissue from her purse.

"You know the strange part?"

"What's that?" Hope asked.

"I don't think I'm actually going to miss him. I think I'm more upset that I couldn't figure out how to make it work." Joy let out a sigh. "And I'm worried for the kids. They're going to be upset."

"I'm sure they will be," Hope said. "But they're adults. They'll be able to handle it." Joy's oldest was twenty-six, and the youngest was twenty-two.

Joy nodded. "You're probably right." Then she let out a big breath and said, "Enough of that. I don't want to think about Paul anymore. Let's get down to business. What do you have for us?"

Hope glanced at Grace. Grace raised her eyebrows and shrugged slightly as if to say that if Joy was ready to move on, it was time to move on.

"Okay then. Grace, were you able to get a list of new residents in town?" Hope asked.

"You know I could get into big trouble for taking this list from the database, right?" Grace asked as she passed over the names of people who'd used her agency to either purchase or rent space in Premonition Pointe over the previous few months.

"I just want to use this list to cross reference who was at Lucas's open house. And then we'll burn it, okay?" Hope asked.

"That's fair." Grace grabbed another cookie and sat back with her coffee mug.

"I'll read the names off and, Hope, you can scan the guest book," Joy said, taking Grace's list. "We'll go one by one."

"Sounds good." Hope grabbed a pen and they got to work.

An hour later, they had the list narrowed down to three people: an interior designer named Vincent Valencia, a freelance writer named Lanie Barnes, and an artist named Crosby Quinn.

"None of these people scream hardened drug criminal," Hope said with a sigh.

Grace looked at the list. "I helped Crosby find his studio space. He's a sweet, shy guy who mostly paints seascapes. He's showing his work at North Star Gallery."

"And Lanie joined the Arts Market co-op. As vice-president, it's my job to look over each application," Joy said. "She makes felted affirmation witches. They say things like *Be your own witch* and *Confidence makes the witch stronger* and *Love your inner witch.* They're very sweet."

Hope pressed her fingertips to her temples. "Vincent is an old friend of Lance's. He's been an interior designer for years, and he moved here to be with his boyfriend and to slow down and enjoy the beach. Do you know what this means?"

"We just wasted an hour instead of getting out and talking to everyone on the list?" Grace asked.

"You got it," Hope said. "If any of these three are involved in moving drugs, I'll run naked down Main Street declaring how brilliant they are. I mean, talk about a convincing cover."

"Be careful with your declarations," Joy said, her voice full of mirth. "You never know. Maybe the reason they've been able to fly under the radar is because they don't even come close to giving off criminal vibes."

"Yeah, any one of them could be the kingpin drug dealer of the California coastal towns," Grace added.

Hope rolled her eyes at her friends. "Ha-ha. Very funny. To make you two jokers happy, we can stop in on them and I'll try to listen in on their thoughts. But if any of them turn out to be dirty pervs who subject me to their depravity, I blame you."

"If they're dirty pervs, that might be a reason to look closer," Joy said, pumping her eyebrows.

"I think we'll leave that to you," Grace said, laughing as she gathered up their mugs and took them to the kitchen. "For now, it looks like we need to head downtown and let our bestie spy on some folks."

CHAPTER NINE

*H*ope led the way into Magical Touch, a co-op design studio that was on the square across from city hall. The showroom was decorated in all white with touches of turquoise and pale yellow. Everything about the place screamed beachy elegance.

"Good afternoon," a familiar looking redhead said from behind the desk. "How can I help you ladies today? Do you have an appointment?"

"Oh, no. We're just out window shopping," Grace said. "Our girl here, Joy, is looking for a home makeover. You know, out with the old, in with the new, and we thought we'd see if Vincent and Walt could help her out."

"Well, they are two designers. They don't usually work on jobs together unless it's a special circumstance. One specializes in modern design and the other in contemporary. Do you have a preference?" the receptionist asked.

"Um, I don't know. I kinda like the furniture from Against the Grain. Whichever works with that esthetic," Joy said.

Hope smiled to herself. She just loved her friends. Joy hadn't wasted even one moment before bringing up Lucas's shop.

"Oh, Lucas King's work," the redhead said, her voice suddenly turning husky, making it sound like she wanted to have a love affair with one of his end tables. "That man is *very talented.*"

Uh, what? Hope thought and immediately zeroed in on the woman. She recognized her now. The woman was one of Gigi's neighbors, and she'd practically stalked Lucas at his opening before he'd brushed her off. The memory had Hope giving the woman a fake smile. "I hear he's off the market."

"He is?" she asked, surprised. "That's news to me considering we have a date on Friday night."

"Uh-oh," Grace breathed.

"*You're* dating Lucas?" Hope asked breathily as if she'd been gut-punched. Had Lucas actually asked the redhead out?

"Yeah. Oh!" she said, her eyes brightening. "Maybe you heard rumors about us and that's why you thought he was off the market. Well, I wouldn't say it's official, but after Friday, who knows?" She shrugged one shoulder and winked, making her intentions very clear. "Goddess knows I deserve a hottie after the jackass I divorced last year. He made good money, but he was way too tightfisted for my tastes. I just hope Lucas is good about taking care of his woman, because I'm not really cut out for working. You know what I mean?"

Hope was so tense there was no chance she was going to be able to access her telepathy. Not after learning that the redhead had her hooks in Lucas. She peered at the woman's nametag. "Listen, Serena, as lovely as it is to hear about your love life, perhaps you can let us know if the designers are in?"

"Oh, sorry." She giggled, and suddenly Hope got a flash of the woman running her hand down Lucas's chest as he stared down at her with an unreadable expression. The vision disappeared just as quickly, leaving Hope agitated and on the verge of biting the woman's head off. "Let's see. Vincent is here, but he's with a client. And Walt is out on an appointment." She turned to Joy. "But I can set something up with them if you want."

"Can I meet with them together?" Joy asked. "Just so I can get a sense of who I might want to work with."

"Sure. How about Friday at ten?"

They set up the appointment while Hope tried her best to see if she could dive into Serena's thoughts. But as soon as she did, all she got were flashes of Lucas in various stages of undress. The only saving grace was that it was obvious the woman hadn't seen him with his clothes off. Hope knew the images were only in the woman's imagination because Lucas's tattoo was missing and so was the jagged scar from when he'd had his appendix out. Not to mention he had an eight pack, not a six pack.

After realizing that Serena and Lucas hadn't taken their relationship past the flirtation phase, she leaned over the counter and said, "I remember you from the open house at Against the Grain. You were there, right?"

"Sure. That's where Lucas and I met."

Of course it was. Although if she recalled correctly, he hadn't given her the time of day. She wondered how Serena had wrangled a dinner invitation. "What did you think of his gallery? Sweet spot, right?"

"Sure." Serena frowned. "I guess. I mean, his work is nice,

but I think we all know Lucas is the main draw. That man is just so dreamy."

Hope had to refrain from rolling her eyes. Serena was far too focused on getting into Lucas's pants for Hope to seriously consider she was part of a drug running ring. "He sure is," Hope said. "Good luck on that date Friday." She turned to Grace and Joy. "Ready?"

They both nodded.

"It was nice meeting you, Serena," Hope forced out.

"See you Friday," Joy added.

Grace waved, and the three of them piled out onto the street.

"Well, that was—" Grace started.

"Brutal," Joy said, cutting her off. "Hope, are you all right?"

"I'm perfect," Hope said, spotting the mayor sitting on a bench under an oak tree while she sipped an iced coffee. "I'll be right back."

She left her friends standing on the sidewalk and crossed the square to where Iris Hartsen was sitting. "Mayor," Hope said, holding her hand out. "It's nice to see you."

The mayor glanced up and smiled as she took Hope's hand. "Ms. Anderson. What brings you to the square in the middle of the day?"

Hope waved at her friends. "We're helping Joy make some redecorating decisions. I saw you here and thought I'd say hello and thank you for making an appearance at the Against the Grain open house. I know Lucas really appreciates the support."

She gave Hope her trademark warm smile, the same one that got her elected with seventy percent of the vote. "I wouldn't have missed it. It's always a pleasure to welcome new business partners to the town." *Especially one that fits in perfectly with our plans.*

Hope almost asked, *What plans?* But then she realized the mayor hadn't said that last part out loud. She blinked. She couldn't possibly be referring to moving drugs, could she? The mayor had worked hard to implement a free drug rehab program in the city a few years back. Surely she couldn't be involved in supplying anyone with illegal substances.

"That rocking chair I bought is just to die for. Did you know my daughter is having a baby?" the mayor asked.

"No, I didn't. Congratulations. That's exciting," Hope said. Images of the woman sitting in the rocking chair flickered in Hope's mind, making her smile. How could she have ever suspected her of being involved in a drug ring? Even the mere thought made her feel foolish.

"It is. I can't wait to hold that little girl in my arms while I rock her in that chair. Lucas is delivering it next week for the nursery. I know it's a little extravagant, but it's for my grandbaby, so it's worth it."

"I can't think of a better reason," Hope said.

They chatted for a few more minutes, and then Hope joined her friends back on the sidewalk in front of Magical Touch.

"Any dirt on Iris?" Grace asked, unable to hold back a chuckle. "Do we need to call in the DEA to raid the mayor's office?"

"Shut it, Valentine. It always pays to make nice with the mayor, especially one who always seems to be in need of an event organizer," Hope said.

"Right." Grace pushed her windblown auburn hair out of her eyes, and said, "So to recap, we've interviewed a desperate ex-housewife and the mayor, who likely would win Miss Congeniality in any competition she ever entered. Are we making progress yet?"

Hope groaned. "This is going to take forever. There are like forty more people on the list, and not a lot of them have storefronts." She eyed Joy. "How do you feel about talking to Gabrielle, the lifestyle reporter for the *Premonition Pointe News?*"

"Sure," she said with a shrug. "Gabrielle and I are friendly. She does all the writeups for the Art Market shows in town. We talk at least a couple times a month."

"Good. Try to find out if she's heard any rumors about increased drug activity in town, and if so, see if she has any contacts over at the sheriff's office. Maybe put a bug in her ear if she seems interested in doing a little digging."

"I'm on it." Joy pulled her phone out, and in a few seconds, she had the reporter on the phone. "Gabrielle, hi! Listen, I wanted to find out if you had any info on the young man who overdosed in the Pointe of View Café yesterday. Hope and I were there when it happened, and I just can't stop thinking about him. I hope he's all right." She walked a short distance away and paused in the shade under an awning.

"She's good," Grace said.

"Very good," Hope agreed. "You know who we need to talk to next?"

"Lucas?" Grace asked, her eyes sparkling with amusement.

Hope ignored her cheeky answer. They didn't need to talk about how much it bothered her to find out Lucas had a date. Besides, Hope had *two* dates that weekend. She had no right to be upset about anything Lucas did. She cleared her throat. "We need to go see Gigi. All of her neighbors were there."

"Rich neighbors," Grace added. "Now that I think about it, that's probably where we should've started."

Hope nodded. "It makes more sense than investigating the guitarist or Kevin Landers."

Grace threw her head back and laughed. "Can you imagine Kevin as a drug kingpin? For all his talk, I don't think he's ever once fired anyone. And he pawns practically all his work off on his assistant. The man is allergic to paperwork. He'd be toppled in less than a week."

"I suppose we do need to talk to the guitarist, too. But I suspect anything I pick up from her with my telepathy will be exactly like Serena's thoughts."

"Oh, gods. Was it that bad?" Grace asked, her face pinched in sympathy.

"It was until I realized she'd never seen him naked. Then I was able to let those visions go," Hope admitted. "I gotta tell you, it sucks hard having to hear about him dating."

"I'm sure he feels the same." Grace pointed across the square at two men standing in front of city hall. "Looks like Lucas just found out about your date with Matt."

Hope followed Grace's gaze and saw the two men standing together on the sidewalk. Lucas met her gaze, scowled, and then turned his ire on Matt, who immediately held his hands up in a *stop* motion and started backing away slowly.

"Oh hell," Hope muttered and started to stride toward them.

CHAPTER TEN

"You can forget about that custom dining room table." Lucas's expression was stormy, and by the way his fists were curled into balls, he looked like he wanted to deck Matt.

"Hey, man. Let's slow down a minute," Matt said, running a hand through his silver hair. "I didn't know there was something going on between you and Hope. It's just dinner."

"There isn't anything going on between us," Hope insisted as she came to a stop beside Matt. What the hell was going on here? Were they really fighting over her? She narrowed her eyes at Lucas. "What exactly did you tell him?"

Lucas shifted his attention to hold her gaze. "Weeks ago, when he asked what I was doing back in town, I told him I was here to take care of my mother and to repair my relationship with you."

"Lucas," she said with a sigh. But before she could go on, Matt interrupted them.

"You said your ex. Not once did you mention Hope's

name," Matt insisted. "Dude, I never would've stepped on your toes like that had I known."

Matt frowned at him. "How could you not know Hope is my ex? Everyone knows that."

He shrugged. "I'm new in town, remember? And I just spent the last few months with my kids and their families at the beach. How would I know Hope is your ex?"

"Um, excuse me," Hope interjected. She had an intense desire to punch one or both of them. "I am not a piece of property for someone to claim."

"Of course, you aren't," Lucas said automatically. Matt nodded his agreement.

"Then why would it matter if I'm your ex?" she asked Lucas. Then she turned to Matt. "And why wouldn't you have asked me out if you'd known that? We're not together. We haven't been since the last time he ran back to the east coast. It's been years." She turned again, this time jabbing her finger into Lucas's chest. "I am free to date whomever I want. You hear me? You. Left. Me. Twice. If you think there's something between us still, you're delusional."

Lucas wrapped his hand around hers and pulled her in closer to him. "There's always going to be something more between us, Hope. And you're lying to yourself if you think otherwise."

Her breath caught, and she couldn't help it when her gaze landed on his mouth. Even though she was furious, her tongue darted out, wetting her lips in anticipation. *Dammit. Why was this so hot?*

Fire blazed in his eyes, and he started to dip his head as he leaned in for the kiss.

She placed a hand on his chest and shoved him back. "You're full of shit. Don't think I haven't heard about your date on Friday night. If you were so determined to put things back together with me, then why are you taking what's-her-face, Serena, to dinner on Friday night?" She gestured awkwardly toward the design shop across the square.

"What? I don't have a date on Friday. And who's Serena?" Lucas asked.

Hope rolled her eyes. "Don't play dumb. The pretty redhead from the open house the other night? She came onto you then. Don't deny it. I saw everything." She was so angry with him she neglected to say that she saw him dismiss her. But had he really? If he was taking her out on Friday, they must've talked later.

He frowned. "I don't remember a redhead. Unless you're talking about the guitarist. But I certainly didn't ask her out." He glanced again at the interior design store, and recognition lit in his silver gaze. "Oh, now I know who you're talking about. The assistant to the two designers, right?"

"Yeah, that one," she said dryly. "Poor thing. She doesn't know what she's getting into."

"I'm not taking her out on Friday. She came into the store to place an order yesterday, and while she was there, she mentioned they have a happy hour at Abalone. I thanked her for the tip and said I'd have to try it out. I think she said something about dropping by and maybe having a drink, but it sure as hell isn't a date. Not like the one you have with Mr. Beach House here." He nodded to Matt.

"I think maybe the date isn't such a good idea," Matt interjected. "Hope, it really looks like you could use some space so that you and Lucas can figure out whatever it is that's going on here. I'm not really interested in being in the middle of someone else's drama."

"There's nothing going on—" Hope started

"That's a great idea, Matt," Lucas said, cutting her off.

"I'm sorry." Matt gave Hope an apologetic smile. "I just know better than to step in the middle of something." He offered his hand to Lucas, and when they shook, Matt said, "Good luck, man."

"Thanks." Lucas nodded to him and then turned back to Hope and said, "Now, about Friday."

"What about it?" she spat out, her blood boiling. "Looks like I'm going to be ordering a pizza now instead of eating oysters, clams, and halibut. Thanks to you. How dare you interfere—"

"Let me take you out," he said. "Abalone or anywhere else you want to go."

"You want me to go on a date with you?" she asked incredulously as she pushed her windswept hair out of her face. The ocean breeze had picked up, and the scent of sea salt washed over her, making a slew of memories hit her all at once. That always happened when the wind picked up. They'd had their first kiss on the beach one afternoon right before a storm. They'd had their first date at the cliff in his pickup, where they'd laid in the back of his truck and stared at the stars. And the night he'd left her for the east coast, they'd sat on the rocks as the water crashed below while they spent their last few minutes together.

"Yes. I want you to go on a date with me. Since I ruined your plans, let me make it up to you." He flashed her that easy smile that had melted her resolve so many times before. It didn't do the trick this time. She was still mad that he thought he had any say in who she dated. How dare he? Normally that would've been enough to tell him to screw off, but the thought of him meeting up with Serena for happy hour made her swallow a groan. Just thinking about the two of them together was enough to make her stomach turn. "Fine. You can buy me dinner on Friday, but only because you owe me. It isn't a date. It's an apology."

His smile widened to a grin and his eyes twinkled with amusement. "You can call it whatever you want, Hope. I'll pick you up at seven." *But we both know it's a date.*

Hope wondered if he'd projected his last thought just to get under her skin. Probably, and it made her want to wipe the smug smile right off his face. "You're infuriating."

"I know." He leaned in and kissed her on the cheek then shoved his hands in his pockets and walked away, whistling as he went.

Hope turned around to head back to her friends, but they'd already caught up with her.

Grace let out a low whistle. "Wow, Hope. You have your hands full with that one. He has all the charm and sex appeal he had back in the day, but now his game is off the charts. I can't believe he just got you to agree to dinner after all of that. How the heck are you going to navigate this minefield?"

Hope threw up her hands. "I have no idea."

Joy patted her on the back. "At least he won't be with Serena."

"Why do you think I agreed?" Hope asked with a sad chuckle. "I'm a complete mess, aren't I?"

"I wouldn't say complete," Grace said, linking her arm through Hope's. "Maybe just a small one. Come on. Let's take a break from sleuthing and find you something to wear on Friday. If you're going to let him take you out, then we need to make sure you're devastatingly gorgeous."

"Grace, that's not necessary," Hope said, even as she let her friend pull her along toward their favorite boutique.

"Oh, yes, it is," Joy said. "Besides, we're going anyway. If I'm going to give Tinder a chance, I'm going to need something better than my long cotton skirts and fitted T-shirts."

"But you look great in those skirts and T-shirts," Hope insisted.

"I don't think hippy mom is the look I'm going for," Joy said with determination. "Now come on. It's time to sex it up a bit."

Hope and Grace exchanged a concerned glance. This wasn't the Joy they were used to. And Hope was worried her friend was diving headfirst into something she wasn't nearly ready for.

But Joy strode ahead, clearly determined to find a new sexy wardrobe, and who were Hope and Grace to stop her? If she wanted to get her sexy on, then so be it. Hope would just make sure she and Grace were there to pick up the pieces when their friend needed them.

CHAPTER ELEVEN

*H*ope put her Toyota Highlander in Park across the street from Gigi Martin's Victorian home on Seaside Drive. The beachfront neighborhood was full of gorgeous houses, most of them owned by well-to-do families from the larger cities. Now that it was early fall, maybe only half appeared to be occupied at the moment, but the street was still full of cars.

"Is Gigi having a party or something?" Joy asked as she glanced around at the expensive vehicles.

"She mentioned something about an informal gathering for the neighborhood," Grace said. "Something about four o'clock cocktails."

"Did someone say cocktails?" Hope asked, ready to down a couple of margaritas. They'd spent nearly two hours at the boutique on Main because Grace and Joy had insisted that Hope try on every single formfitting or low-neckline dress in the place. However, she had found a sexy black wrap dress that made her feel fifteen years younger, so maybe they'd been onto something.

"I could use a drink after that ego-crushing experiment," Joy said as she tied her long blond hair into a neat bun. It always amazed Hope how Joy could quickly look so put together even when she was wearing yoga pants and a *Not today, Satan* T-shirt. She just had that elegant, graceful look about her that Hope had always envied.

"You're kidding right? Your ass looks great in those jeans you bought," Grace said. "And that blouse? It's romantic and sexy. That Tinder date, whoever he is, won't know what hit him."

"Yeah, I like the blouse. I just... Maybe I should join a gym," she said, pressing her palms to her stomach.

Hope just stared at her and then shook her head.

"What?"

"Nothing. I just think you're being a little hard on yourself," Hope said. "You already look amazing, but I fully support joining to get into shape. In fact, I'll do it with you. Spin class, yoga, Pilates. What do you say?"

"Whoa, lady. I was just thinking about some yoga and maybe the elliptical. Spin class? Have you ever done that?" Joy asked.

"I have," Grace said. "It kicked my ass." She laughed. "I went once and never went back. Now I just use the pool."

"The pool really is more my speed," Hope said, leading the way up to Gigi's house. "Too bad none of us have one. Can't you just see the three of us at our cabana while the pool boy wanders around?"

Maybe I should put in a pool. Use Paul's money and hire my own pool boy. Maybe the sexy neighbor a few doors down wants a part-time job. Then I wouldn't need a Tinder date, Joy thought.

Hope suppressed a snicker but turned and gave her two thumbs up.

"Hope!" Joy exclaimed. "Stop reading my thoughts. That's just..." She squeezed her eyes closed and shook her head. "Dammit."

"Oh, I wanna know what dirty thing she was thinking," Grace said, excitement dancing in her eyes. "Was it about a pool boy?"

Hope nodded, this time not bothering to hold back her laughter. "Yep. She's thinking of putting in a pool with Paul's money and hiring the sexy neighbor to service her... uh, pool."

Grace cackled. "I'll be over every day at six. And as payment, I'll keep your bar stocked."

"Stop it," Joy said, laughing with them. "I'm sure the pool boy would be some slightly overweight family man in his fifties, so let's not get too crazy. But I really am considering the pool. I've always wanted one, but Paul said it'd be too much work. Now that he's moved out, he doesn't get a say."

"Good for you," Hope said as she knocked on Gigi's door.

"Yeah. Let me know when you break ground," Grace added. "We'll celebrate."

"Damn straight we will." Joy held her head high and had that look of determination again.

Hope loved to see it. Paul had been bringing her down for far too long. Joy deserved to do something to make herself happy.

The door swung open, and Gigi Martin grinned. "Grace! You made it." She pulled Grace into her gorgeous home. "Hey, Hope. Joy. Follow me. I have drinks out on the deck." *Thank the gods. People to save me from these jackholes,* Gigi thought.

Hope leaned in and whispered to Joy, "She hates her neighbors."

"Really?" Joy whispered back, her eyes wide.

"Yep. Let's go shake things up."

"On it." Joy swept through the French doors out onto the deck and headed straight for the booze.

Hope glanced around and spotted a handful of middle-aged men dressed in Dockers and polo shirts. She imagined all they talked about were their stock portfolios and golf scores. Woo-effing-hoo. This was going to be one dull-ass party. Joy had the right idea.

"What's that?" Hope pointed to Joy's pink drink.

"I have no idea. Tastes like vodka and raspberry. Want one?"

"Sure."

Joy poured her one of the pinktinis and then another for Grace, who was being monopolized by Gigi. Grace took the glass and mouthed *thank you* before turning her attention back to their hostess.

"Let's do this thing," Hope said and eyed a group of five men.

"Where are all the women?" Joy asked. "I didn't realize we were walking into a sausage fest. No wonder Gigi was desperate for a little estrogen."

Hope snickered. Joy was on fire today. Hope was impressed at how she'd rallied after learning that her husband was moving out. It was probably really good for her to have something else to focus on. "I think we're about to find out."

"Well hello there, pretty ladies." A tall man with the build of a linebacker greeted them. He had short blond hair and the kind of smarmy smile that screamed douchecanoe. He scanned Joy, and his expression morphed into the kind of leer Hope had seen on just about every frat boy she'd ever encountered at a college party. *Yoga pants. I'd like to get her into a downward facing dog,* he thought.

Hope wanted to gag. Yep, he was one hundred percent douchebucket.

"Hello, I'm Joy, and this is Hope," Joy said, holding out her hand. "Who might you be?"

"Your date on Friday night." His grin was way too cocky, and everything about the guy gave Hope the creeps.

"Oh, really? I wasn't aware I'd been asked," Joy said, her tone suddenly icy.

Pride swelled in Hope's chest. Joy had been knocked down today, but she wasn't out. And she certainly wasn't going to take this guy's crap.

The man chuckled as if he were used to women pushing back at him. "I like you. Great shirt by the way. I'm Brent Card, owner of the house three doors down. The one with a Maserati out front. Feel free to stop by if you're interested in a dip in my hot tub."

"Why would I do that when Gigi has one right here?" Joy waved at the hot tub in the corner of the deck.

"Oh, it's like that, is it?" he asked, raising one eyebrow.

"Like what?" Joy shot back.

"You like to play hard to get. No problem. I'm up for the challenge." He started talking about his VP sales job at a Bay area pharmaceutical company. Hope focused on him and did her best to open her mind to him. His thoughts were one hundred percent about how great he was. Then as he scanned Joy, he thought, *Surely, once I show her my house and the view from the master bedroom, she'll melt for me just like all the others.*

Hope wanted to gag and actually contemplated pushing him over the deck railing. But there were too many witnesses, and he wasn't worth the hassle of prison. He was so shallow and full of shit that Hope couldn't help wondering how his blue eyes hadn't turned brown yet.

Hope leaned over and whispered to Joy, "As cringeworthy as this guy is, I don't get the sense he's into illegal drugs. Are you going to be okay if I go talk to the others?"

Joy nodded and went back to humoring Brent. Hope was sure she'd get around to asking about the overdoses in town to see if he had anything to say about them.

"Excuse me," Hope said to him. "It was nice to meet you, but I'm going to mingle."

The man barely acknowledged that Hope had said anything and turned his attention back to Joy.

Hope bypassed the other frat boy look-a-likes and made her way over to three men who were leaning against the porch railing and laughing at something one of them had said. One of them was in jeans and a short-sleeved button-down shirt, one had ripped jeans and a form-fitting T-shirt, and the third wore cargo pants and a long-sleeved cotton shirt. They appeared much more down to earth and approachable. "Hello. I'm Hope Anderson, a friend of Gigi's."

"Oh, aren't you adorable," the shortest one with the ripped jeans said, eyeing her. "That cut is fantastic. Who did it?"

Hope smiled at him. He had a genuine smile and bright green eyes that sparkled in the sunlight. Hope liked him instantly. "Lance over at Liminal Space Day Spa. Do you know him?"

"No. Pete and I purchased our vacation home last fall, but

this is the first chance we've had to spend any significant time here." He slipped his arm around the sexy six-foot guy next to him who had a close-cut beard and dark eyes. "We just got here a few days ago, and Gigi was kind enough to host this gathering."

"Hi, I'm Pete," the bearded guy said. He nodded his head toward his partner. "And this is my husband Skyler."

"Hi, nice to meet you both." She shook their hands and then glanced at the third guy, who was wearing the cargo pants. He was tall and thin with a strong jawline and kind blue eyes.

"Hi, I'm Troy," he said.

"Hope. I assume you all live on this street?" she asked.

They all nodded. "Pete and Skyler have the modern gray house at the end," Troy said. "Mine is the three story with the multiple decks right next to theirs."

Hope was impressed. Besides Gigi's Victorian, they were the two nicest homes on the block, and she couldn't help wondering what they all did for a living that they could afford beach front property.

"None of us do," Hope said, waving a hand toward her friends. "Grace is the realtor who sold the house to Gigi. Joy is the vice president of the Arts Market, and I'm an event planner. So if you need someone to organize a birthday, anniversary, holiday party, or something like that, I'm your girl."

"Oh, really," Skyler said, stepping closer to her and slipping his arm through hers. "We definitely need to talk."

"Here we go." Pete rolled his eyes and turned to Troy. "Wanna bet this is about a dog wedding?"

"You mean he was serious about Polly and Drew tying the

knot?" Troy asked, looking intrigued. "I thought that was a joke."

"It was, but you know how he is. When he gets something in his mind, things start to escalate," Pete said, shaking his head.

"If we're going to have puppies, then I think they deserve a ceremony," Skyler insisted. "Right, Hope?"

"Sure." Hope chuckled. "What were you thinking? Beachside?"

"Oh, heavens no." Skyler placed a hand on his chest, looking scandalized. "Have you ever seen a shih tzu at the beach? The sand is a nonstarter. I was actually thinking a ceremony on the cliff, overlooking the sea. Maybe bring in a gazebo or a trellis. Or, oh I know, how about a couple of dogwood trees?"

"All decent possibilities," Hope said, completely amused. She'd organized all kinds of parties before, but never a dog wedding. "Why don't we set up an appointment to get together and see what we can come up with?"

"Yes, let's." He pulled his phone out of his pocket and opened his calendar. Then he laughed. "I'm so used to meetings and deadlines that I keep forgetting that we don't have anything planned while we're here for the next month or so. According to this, I'm free any day."

"Except Friday nights, remember?" Pete said, running his thumb down the back of Skyler's neck.

Skyler flushed as he looked up at his husband and gave him a tender smile. "Friday's, right."

"No problem. I don't usually work on Friday nights either." She winked at them. "Gotta have some time to play, right?"

Skyler nodded. "Date night. That reminds me, where do you recommend for awesome seafood?"

"Abalone," Troy said immediately. "It's a new place, very fresh. The parmesan crusted halibut is my favorite, but they have great fish and chips, too."

Hope nodded. "I've heard nothing but good things about them. Make sure you get a reservation though. It's the hot place to be these days."

Skyler tapped a note into his phone. "Abalone. Got it."

They made an appointment for Monday to discuss details of the dog wedding, and then the four of them stood there awkwardly until Hope said, "So. You guys know I'm an event planner. What do you three do for a living?"

"Pete's a personal finance manager, and I'm a designer," Skyler said. "I have a store in San Francisco and one in Los Angeles. Women's wear and some custom gowns."

"Skyler works very hard, but I finally convinced him to take some time off. So while we're here through October, there will be no work," Pete said. "Just beaches, puppies, and enjoying the outdoors, right babe?"

"Of course. I promised, didn't I?" Skyler leaned in and hugged his husband.

"That's very cool," Hope said. "Do you have an online store? I'd love to check it out."

Skyler handed her a business card. "While you're at it, make sure you take a look at Troy's stuff too. He's a photographer, and his new shots of the coast are incredible."

"Really?" Hope turned to Troy. "Do you show your photos professionally?"

"Yeah," Troy said with a modest shrug. "There are a few galleries in the city that carry them. But I have a pretty good following online and sell a lot of prints through my website. It's easier than dealing with art galleries."

Hope desperately wanted to know his story. How could he afford a three-story, beachfront house in Premonition Pointe if he was selling prints from his website?

"Oh. My. God!" Skyler exclaimed. "Stop being so modest." He rolled his eyes at the photographer. "Troy's work has been in every magazine from here to Paris. He photographs celebrities for national covers. That's how we met. My clothing line was featured in *Off the Rack Magazine*, and Troy did the shoot. He's actually the reason we ended up buying in Premonition Pointe. We did the shoot on the beach here and fell in love with the town."

"That's fantastic. So Troy, you've been here a while. I'm surprised I haven't seen you around," Hope said.

"I spend a lot of time in nature behind my lens," he said.

"Isn't that the truth." Skyler shook his head. "But don't worry. We'll get him out and about. Maybe find him a date. Do you know any eligible locals we can set him up with?"

"Sky…" Troy said with a sigh.

"Um… male or female? Or does it matter?" Hope asked.

"Oh, definitely female," Pete said. "We made the mistake of trying to set him up with one of our friends last year, and let's just say it did not go well."

"That's because you told me it was for a photoshoot," Troy said, glaring at Pete. "If you would've asked me first, I'd have told you I'm into women."

Pete threw his hands up. "How was I supposed to know? You had all those photos of half-naked men."

"That was work for an LGBTQ publication," Troy told Hope.

"Sounds like your work is well-rounded," Hope said, truly fascinated.

"I've heard that before." Troy focused on Pete. "How's your work going? Are you taking time off while you're here, too?"

Pete started talking about still being available for his clients but that he was planning to take as much time off as possible. Then they moved on to discussing the financial markets.

Hope feigned interest while she tried to concentrate on hearing their thoughts. She was starting to feel predatory as she actively tried to spy on them, but the idea of someone else overdosing was worse.

She focused on Troy while Skyler complained about how much time Pete spent on the computer. An image of a young man posing on a balcony flashed in her mind. He was shirtless, his hair windswept and his eyes sleepy as if he'd just woken up. The image was replaced with one of a young woman posed on a rock wearing nothing but an oversized sweatshirt. More models entered his mind, and Hope decided he was planning upcoming shoots.

She shifted her attention to Pete and was rewarded with thoughts of him carrying Skyler back to their house where they could be alone. She shut down her telepathy instantly and told them how nice it was to meet them and that she'd see Skyler next week.

She spent a little bit of time talking to Brent's cohorts. She learned they were friends of his and staying in his house, and they were just as douchey as he was. When she jokingly brought up the idea of them reliving their frat days and teased them about indulging in booze and drugs, they laughed along with her. Then one of them asked if she had a hookup. By the time she left them, she'd had to fend off one who was getting handsy and dodge the request for her number from another one. But as problematic as they were, there wasn't any evidence that they were part of a drug ring.

"Hope, there you are," Grace said when Hope found her chatting in the kitchen with Gigi and Joy. The men had finally left, and it was just the four women remaining in the house.

"You three left me alone with the sausage fest," Hope said, pointing a finger at them. "Not cool. Not cool at all. What happened to our promise about no girl left behind?"

"I tried to get your attention, but you were too busy flirting with Ken," Joy said.

Hope scoffed. "Okay, first of all, I wasn't flirting with anyone. And second... Ken? Are you kidding me? One of those frat boys was named Ken?"

Gigi laughed. "Yep. Ken, Brent, Rip, Todd, and Dawson. Unbelievable, right?"

Hope shook her head. "Yes and no."

They all laughed.

"My hat's off to you, Gigi," Hope said. "It's really something to host a party when you know those dudes are going to show up."

She scoffed. "I invited Skyler, Pete, and Troy. Brent overheard and invited himself. Then he brought his bros." Gigi shuddered. "Thank the goddess they're gone. The spirits of the house weren't too pleased with their presence. That's why I made them stay outside."

Well, that was interesting. Gigi's house was haunted, but the spirits who occupied it had embraced Gigi. They had even stepped up to help her when her ex got violent. So Hope was inclined to trust their judgement. "What happened?"

Gigi shrugged. "When Brent and his boys walked in, the wind picked up, causing the door to slam, and then the house started creaking. It's the warning sign that they are about to start some shit if the person they don't like doesn't leave. I quickly ushered them all outside. Haven't heard a peep since."

Hope made a mental note to do a deep dive into Brent and his boys. The spirits clearly knew something the rest of them didn't. They made plans for the group to get lunch the next week, thanked Gigi for the cocktails, and made their way outside.

"Thanks for the backup," Gigi called as they made their way to Hope's car.

"Anytime," Hope said, meaning it. She really liked Gigi, and once they were in the Highlander, Hope turned to her friends. "I think it's time to invite her to the coven. What do you think? Should we talk to her about it at lunch?"

"I'm in," Grace said. "I love Gigi."

Joy took a deep breath. "I love her, too, but let's be sure about this. Once we vote her in, there's no voting her off the island."

Hope nodded. Joy had a very good point. The coven was their sacred circle. It was a big deal to invite someone in. They needed to trust her implicitly. No one wanted to upset their circle.

"I'm sure," Grace said. "I think she fits right in with us, and maybe more importantly, I think she *needs* our circle. After what happened with her husband when she bought this place, and how she gracefully handled it, I have so much respect and admiration for her."

"Same," Hope said. Gigi's husband had attacked her right

there in her new house when she told him she was buying it. She'd immediately filed for divorce and kicked him right out of her life.

"Okay. I agree," Joy said, smiling. "Just wanted to be sure everyone had thought it through. We'll invite her next week."

CHAPTER TWELVE

"I'm really excited," Joy said, rubbing her hands together. She'd dressed up in her beige wide-legged pants and a form-fitting silk blouse. Her hair was bound in a stylish twist, and Hope thought she looked like an entirely different person than the one who'd shown up at her house in yoga pants a couple of days before.

"You look great," Hope said as they walked across the square toward Magical Touch.

"I think I just needed a few days to get used to my new reality. It's not like Paul was ever home much anyway, right? Now I don't have to cook him dinner or do his laundry. Honestly, it's been a relief to tell you the truth."

Hope eyed her suspiciously. It was obvious that she was trying to convince herself, and Hope wasn't going to challenge her on it. If that's what she needed to do in order to adapt to her new reality, then Hope was all for it. "Have you decided what you want redecorated? Just the bedroom?"

Joy shook her head. "Nope. I'm going for the living room, dining room, and my bedroom. Paul and I picked out the furniture I have now fifteen years ago, and you know I've always hated the dark hardwood. No one should have dark wood at the beach."

"I certainly agree with that." Hope was joining her so that she could try to get a read on Vincent Valencia, the new designer in town, and as long as she was there, she'd check in on his partner Walt Waterman too. If they didn't raise any red flags, she'd leave Joy to it and move on to the other two people on her list, Lanie Barnes, the freelance writer, and Crosby Quinn, the painter. She still thought it was a waste of time, but it had been a couple days since she'd done any work on trying to find the source of the drugs in Premonition Pointe. And since she couldn't stop thinking about the young man who'd overdosed at the café, she felt she had to do something.

"Hey, are you excited about your date tonight, or are you freaking out?" Joy asked.

Hope sighed. "I have no idea." She paused out in front of Magical Touch. "Do you think I've lost my mind accepting a date with Lucas? He's broken my heart twice. I'm just setting myself up to be hurt again, aren't I?"

Joy grabbed her hand and held it between both of her own. "I don't think you've lost your mind. If you ask me, you and Lucas are soul mates. I don't know if that means you're destined to be together or not, but I do know you'll always be in each other's lives one way or another. It's okay to explore what that might look like."

Hope blew out a breath. "I think I'd die if I had to see him date someone else."

"If he does, just kick him in the junk, rendering him defective. That would teach him," Joy said with a smirk.

"That would be one way to handle it," Hope agreed with a

nod. "Is that what you did to Paul after he told you he was done?"

"Ha! I would've, but he's already defective. So I didn't waste my energy." She pulled the door open and strode in.

Hope followed her friend into the studio and didn't know if she should laugh or cry. It made her so angry the way Paul had treated her friend. If he'd agreed to counseling or even tried to meet her halfway, that would've been one thing. But he'd just given up on her and their marriage. Joy deserved better.

"Oh, hello," Serena said, glaring at Hope. "I didn't realize *you* were going to be here today." *If Vincent wasn't already pissed at me, I'd throw that man-stealing rat out right on her ass,* the redhead thought.

Hope cracked a smile, and in an achingly sweet voice she said, "I'm so sorry about your plans tonight. I guess Lucas didn't realize you were asking him out. Better luck next time, huh?"

Serena gripped her pencil so hard it actually snapped in two.

"I have an appointment at ten," Joy said.

"Ahh, here she is," a man sang out from behind them. "Walt told me you were like a ray of sunshine. Look at you, so chic. I can't wait to see what we can do for you." He held his hand out to Joy. "I'm Vincent. And it's a pleasure to meet you."

"Oh, you're a charmer, aren't you? I'm Joy Lansing, and this is my friend Hope Anderson." They all shook hands, and then Vincent ushered them into a conference room where Walt was waiting with a couple of champagne flutes.

"Good morning, ladies. It's been a while, hasn't it, Hope?" he said, already reaching for a champagne bottle.

"It has. How have you been?" Hope had organized a few holiday events for Walt in the past.

"Good. Mimosa?" He held the champagne bottle up.

"If you're having one," she said.

"Of course." He turned to Joy. "One for you as well?"

"Definitely." She grinned, and for once, Hope thought she really did look happy. "Today is all about celebrating new beginnings."

Walt poured three glasses of mimosas. After he passed two of the glasses to Hope and Joy, he held his up and said, "To new beginnings."

They toasted with him, while Vincent mimed toasting with an invisible glass.

"No mimosa for you this morning, Vincent?" Hope asked.

"None for me," he said, cheerily. "Sixteen years sober. I'll celebrate later when we break out the cupcakes."

"Cupcakes? Where?" Hope insisted, glancing around.

He laughed and opened a pastry box and handed her a fancy pink cupcake with a sugar daisy on top.

"You are my new best friend," Hope said, taking the cupcake and abandoning the mimosa.

"You're my kind of girl," Vincent said, grabbing his own cupcake and joining her. Once he bit into the sinful treat, his eyes rolled to the back of his head and he thought, *This is perfection. Design, new friends, and sugar. It's the perfect way to start the workday.*

Hope loved him instantly. "I wasn't kidding about the new best friend crack. You're stuck with me now," she said.

He chuckled. "And here I thought I'd never know the way to a woman's heart." He winked at Walt, who smiled at him. "I've been working on pleasing that one for the last two years."

"Is that how long you two have been together? Romantically, I mean?" Joy asked.

"Yep," Walt said. "I finally convinced this one to move up here a few months ago, and life has never been better. Hiking in the woods, walks on the beach, shopping for fabrics on Sunday mornings. Now if I can just talk him into that King Charles Spaniel I've always wanted, then life would be perfect."

"Oh, Vincent, let the man get a dog," Hope said, giving him her best puppy dog eyes.

Vincent groaned. "You can't be my new best friend if you're gonna take Walt's side on this. All I wanted was some time to settle in before we add a puppy to the mix."

They continued to banter about puppies, until finally Joy interrupted and insisted they get to work on redecorating her home.

It didn't take long for Hope to determine that the two older designers had about as much chance of being involved in the drug business as Joy did. After she gave her opinion on a couple of Joy's choices, she excused herself and made the rounds of the town.

The painter, Crosby Quinn, turned out to be a quiet man who rented a room above a garage, and in addition to painting seascapes for the North Star Gallery, he also drew caricatures on the square on the weekends for extra cash. Lanie Barnes was a young twenty-something who shopped at the secondhand clothing store and clipped coupons just to make her rent while trying to build her portfolio as a freelance writer.

By the time Hope got home, she'd made zero progress on the drug investigation, but she'd purchased one of Crosby's paintings and had traded Lanie a one-hundred-dollar gift card for Pointe of View Café in exchange for any information she could dig up on possible drug dealers infiltrating Premonition Pointe.

"Hope, is that you?" Angela called the moment Hope walked in her front door.

"Who else would it be?" Hope called back as she headed into the kitchen to make herself a cup of coffee.

Angela appeared in the doorway of the kitchen and crossed her arms over her chest. "There's no need to be snappy. I just wanted to say hi."

Guilt washed over Hope like it did so often when she was dealing with her mother. She didn't know how to curb her irritation with Angela. It seemed all her mother needed to do was be present to set Hope off. "I'm sorry, Mom. That was uncalled for."

Angela moved into the kitchen and reached for the cookie jar. "Don't worry about it. I know we're still adjusting."

Part of the issue was that Hope didn't know exactly *what* she was adjusting to. "Uh, Mom?"

"Yeah?" Angela took a bite of the chocolate chip cookie and rested her elbows on the counter.

"What's your plan?"

"Plan for what?" she asked.

Hope rolled her eyes. She knew by now that her mom was almost always listening in on her thoughts.

"I think you need to say it, Hope. Or we're never going to move past this stage. Don't assume I always know what you're thinking. I might hear some things, but I don't hear it all and I don't want to assume anything."

"Fine," Hope blurted. "How long are you staying?"

"Here in Premonition Pointe or here in your house?" she asked.

"Both."

A flicker of pain flashed in her mom's eyes, but she stood up straight and said, "I'm back in Premonition Pointe permanently. As for how long I'm staying here, that all depends on you."

Hope groaned. "Can't you just give me a straight answer? What depends on me?"

"I'm here until you don't need me anymore." She smiled serenely at Hope and started to move toward the living room. "Oh, one more thing."

"What's that?" Hope asked, practically seething. What the hell did 'until you don't need me anymore' even mean?

"I was at Bird's Eye Bakery this morning, and I overheard something I think you might be interested in."

Hope raised one eyebrow and waited her out.

"I didn't see who it was because the place was very busy. But I overheard someone worrying about the overdoses, and then they said they were trying to find a way to get out of the business. It seemed very much like, whoever this person is, he or she doesn't want to be involved and is maybe being blackmailed or forced into it."

Hope blinked, trying to take in what her mother had just said. "You heard this, but you have no idea who it was?"

"That's right." She walked into the living room, and Hope was certain she projected her next thought. *If you want my help to track this down, all you have to do is ask.*

Hope sat on one of her kitchen stools, knowing she should call her mother back right that instant. Even though Angela hated her ability and it had turned into more of a disability than an asset, the truth was she had an extraordinary skill. Over the last week, Hope had learned that it took work for her to hear people's thoughts. In fact, after actively trying to listen in on their thoughts, she was left feeling drained.

But her mother? She didn't even need to try. In fact, for her it was the opposite. She had to actively try to block thoughts, or she got overwhelmed.

"Oh hell," Hope muttered under her breath. Then she called out, "Mom?"

"I'm headed to the beach," Angela called back.

Hope shook her head and couldn't help the tiny smile that made her lips twitch. Her mother was going to make her work for it. "Do you want company?"

Her mom appeared in the doorway again. "Are you actually offering to take a walk with me?"

"Yes." Hope nodded, hating that her mom looked so surprised and so hopeful. Had Hope really been so bad that it was a surprise that she was willing to spend any time with her mother at all? There was no question. The answer was yes. She'd let her resentment get the better of her and hadn't taken the time to try to understand what had happened from her mother's point of view. She hadn't wanted to; she was still too hurt.

"Okay then. Ready?"

"Yep." Hope put her coffee mug down, grabbed her sweatshirt, and joined her mother on her walk to the beach. They were quiet until they were walking barefoot along the seashore. Hope zipped up her hoodie, trying to keep warm in the cool breeze, and said, "I owe you an apology."

"No you don't, bunny," Angela said, slipping her arm through Hope's.

"That's generous of you, but we both know it isn't true. I

should have filled you in on the drug issue in town instead of just letting you read my thoughts, and I should've asked for your help."

Angela stopped in her tracks. "You want my help?"

"Yes. You hear everything. If anyone can crack this, it's you."

Her mom chuckled. "You know I get overwhelmed with thoughts, right? It's not like I can go out all day and listen to everyone. I'd lose my mind."

"But could you go for an hour a day? To the café or the bakery? And just keep a mental ear out?" Hope asked.

Angela gave her daughter a slow smile and then pulled her into a tight hug. "I'd love to, Hope. Anything for my girl."

CHAPTER THIRTEEN

*N*erves had Hope anxiously pacing her living room. It was five minutes to seven. Five minutes until Lucas was supposed to show up to take her to dinner. What had she been thinking, agreeing to this date? Their history proved that she couldn't stay away from him. The last time he'd come back, they'd ended up in bed together after only twenty-four hours. At least this time she'd managed some semblance of self-control. But how long would that last? She'd already proved to herself that she wasn't going to let another woman take her spot by his side.

She sighed and smoothed the fabric of her black wrap dress. It did wonders to show off her curves and made her feel sexy and confident. At least she wouldn't be self-conscious about the way she looked or the few extra pounds she'd put on over the years. Normally she never worried about those things. But he'd known her when she was a teenager and a vibrant, active twenty-something, and at forty-six, there was no way she'd be living up to her former youthful appearance.

The knock on the door startled her out of her thoughts. She sucked in a cleansing breath and went to greet the love of her life.

Hope opened the door to find Lucas standing on her porch wearing black jeans and a blazer over a black Nirvana T-shirt. If that wasn't enough, he was holding a bundle of daisies. Memories flooded her brain of the night he'd taken her out on their first date. He'd shown up in the very same outfit, holding the very same flowers, and had told her that night that one day he was going to marry her.

Tears stung her eyes, and she forced herself to blink them back even as her heart melted into a puddle of goo. This was too much.

"Good evening, Hope," he said, leaning in and kissing her on the cheek. "You look fantastic. Even better than you did at seventeen."

She shook her head slightly, doing her best to climb out from under his spell. "You're playing dirty, King." She waved a hand up and down, indicating his outfit, and then eyed the flowers. "Do you think this is charming?"

Yes, and so do you, he thought as he nodded.

Dammit. He was right. It was really effing charming. She wanted to step right into his arms and kiss the hell out of him. Instead, she took the daisies from him and spun on her heel, not even bothering to invite him in.

She heard his footsteps behind her and wasn't surprised. They were way past formalities. "Let me just put these in some water and then we can go."

"No rush. The reservation is for seven-thirty."

As she filled a vase with water, she watched him from the corner of her eye. He hadn't been in her house in five years. She wondered what he saw. Did he notice the changes she'd made? The cottage hadn't been much when she'd purchased it over ten years ago, and she'd slowly but surely been having it remodeled and updated. She was proud of her little space that was just a few blocks from the beach. Of course she'd always wanted a house with land, but she wasn't going to be able to afford that in Premonition Pointe while running an event planning business.

"Your kitchen is cozy, Hope," he said, glancing around. "I love that farmhouse sink and butcherblock countertop. I was thinking of putting something similar in my house."

She tilted her head and studied him. "Remodeling, huh? Are you doing a lot of work on your house?"

He shrugged. "If it's going to be my forever home, then yes. If not, I'll only do what's necessary to resell."

"If?" Hope tensed. "So, how long are you staying in Premonition Pointe this time?" The words were clipped and came out sounding much more hostile than she'd anticipated.

He frowned and shoved his hands in his pockets. "I thought I was clear that I was planning to stay here for good. Why else would I open a retail storefront?"

"But you just said you didn't know if the house would be your forever home. Why wouldn't it be? It's gorgeous." In fact, Hope had always wanted the very house he'd bought. If she'd had the resources, she'd have scooped it up herself.

He stared down at her and gave her a slow smile. "I think we both already know that I bought that house because of you."

It was her turn to frown. He was right. She did know he'd purchased that house because of her. How many times had they talked about living there together when they were younger? She wasn't dense. It was all part of his plan to try to get back together with her. But she wasn't going to acknowledge that. Not now. Not yet. She wasn't ready. "You bought it because you needed a place for you and your mother." He'd moved back to town because his mother had early stage dementia. "How is Bell by the way?" Hope asked, feeling like a jerk for not asking sooner.

He gave her a look that said he knew exactly what she was doing, but just like her, he let it go for the moment. "She's doing fairly well. The doctor has her on a new medication that's helping her retain her lucidity. She gardens and paints a lot these days. And we got a golden retriever. They take walks around the property. Her friend Hattie stays with her a lot when I'm not home. They're having girls' night tonight."

"That's good. I need to stop by and see her," Hope said. Bell King used to live a few blocks from Hope's house, and they'd relaxed on Bell's porch while they talked over coffee a few times a month. But since she'd moved in with Lucas, Hope had only seen her once. And she missed her. They'd always been close even after Lucas had left town. Mrs. K. had been a second mother to Hope. That guilt was back, poking at her conscience. Why had she let her feelings about Lucas cloud her relationship with his mother?

"I'm sure she'd love that. She asks about you a lot. Always wants to know how your business is doing and who you're dating."

Hope snorted. "She asks *you* who I'm dating?"

He nodded, pursing his lips to indicate he was not amused. "Apparently you have a robust dating life. She misses your stories."

"I don't date *that* much," Hope mumbled. That was a lie. Hope hadn't had any serious boyfriends. Not since Lucas anyway. But she did date for fun quite a bit. Or had until Lucas walked back into town.

"Whatever you say, Hope." He grabbed her hand. "Ready for dinner?"

A tingle that was a direct result of his touch started at her fingertips and ran up her arm. She shivered slightly and pulled away. "Yeah. Let's go before we miss our reservation." Hope grabbed her sweater and led the way outside to Lucas's truck.

He opened the door for her, and once they were on their way to town, silence settled between them.

Hope considered trying to open her mind to listen to what he was thinking but quickly shut that idea down. That just always felt like a violation, and to be honest, she wasn't sure she even wanted to know what he was thinking. Not after that comment about her dating life. She was sure he hadn't stopped dating. It had been fifteen years since they'd last been together, after all.

"You're thinking too much over there," he said as he pulled his truck into a parking spot at Abalone.

"Yeah? I could say the same about you," she said.

He glanced over at her. "If I didn't know better, I'd think you were listening in on my thoughts."

"What makes you think I'm not?" she asked.

He chuckled. "Because if you were, I'm certain you wouldn't be silent right now."

The curiosity almost killed her, but her determination won out. She didn't want to force her way into his private thoughts because she knew he was taunting her. Whatever he was thinking, he wanted her to listen. But she wasn't going to take the bait. If he wanted her to know something, he was going to have to spit it out on his own.

Lucas placed a hand on the small of her back as he led her inside the restaurant. It was right on the waterfront, with gorgeous views of the sun setting over the Pacific Ocean, but the restaurant itself wasn't all that fancy. Most of the patrons were in jeans, though they'd dressed their looks up a little with button-down shirts or blouses. The building was from the early 1900s and had old wood floors and rustic lanterns for lighting.

After they were seated and had ordered drinks, Hope glanced at Lucas. "How's business? Any leads after the open house?"

"Actually, yes. A few. I have a realtor from a few towns over who signed a contract for furniture rental for staging houses, and the buyer from Lux and Comfort sent a contract over this morning. Looks like that's going to be an interesting arrangement. And the mayor's husband stopped in to purchase a side table, and while he was there, he told me his company can take care of the sawdust from the workroom. They'll compress it and make it into kindling or something. It's a win-win for both of us."

"Good! I'm so glad," Hope said, meaning it. She really did want him to succeed, no matter what happened between them.

"It's because of all your hard work, so thank you." He reached across the table and brushed a lock of her dark hair out of her eyes. "This is probably unprofessional of me to be taking my event planner out for dinner, isn't it?"

She chuckled. "No doubt, but we never were much for the rules, were we?"

The mood shifted between them again, and the sudden sexual tension was just too much. The way he was looking at her, like he wanted to devour her, was overwhelming. She had to glance away to keep from throwing herself at him right there at the table.

"Are you happy, Hope?" Lucas asked.

She jerked her head up and stared at him. Finally, she asked, "Why?"

"I've always wondered if you were happy with your decision to stay in Premonition Pointe. If you ever wondered what would've happened if you'd come with me fifteen years ago."

Anger bubbled in her chest. That was not a question she wanted to answer. It wasn't even one she'd been willing to ask herself. It was too painful. "Of course I'm happy. I have a successful business, great friends, a great home. It's a good life."

He nodded. "I can see that. I could say the same for the life I built back East, but there was always something missing."

Hope averted her gaze and grabbed a sourdough roll from the breadbasket that had been placed on the table. "You wanted a wife?"

"No."

When he didn't continue, she reluctantly met his gaze. The intensity that he was reflecting back at her made her nervous, and she went for the joke instead of encouraging this conversation. "A private jet? So you can join the mile-high club?"

He chuckled as she knew he would. It was something they'd joked about when they were kids. He'd say he was going to be so successful that he'd buy her one of the houses on the beach. And she'd say she didn't need that. Just a jet so they could join the mile-high club without having to stuff themselves in a bathroom on a commercial airline. "I'd only want that if we were still together. I can't imagine joining the mile-high club with anyone other than you."

Well dammit. Why did he have to go and say that? "You're just being a sap now."

"You're right. I am." He reached across the table and took her free hand in his own. "Hope, you're what my life's been missing. The first time I left you, I was young and so were you. We both had college, and I know I broke my promise when I said I'd stay here and go to the state school with you, but I couldn't pass up my chance to go to the school of my dreams. You know that, right?"

She nodded. "Of course I do". She wasn't so selfish that she'd expected him to give up a scholarship just because he'd promised to stay in Premonition Pointe with her. "But that doesn't mean you didn't break my heart when you left and said we'd do long distance and then changed your mind two months later."

He winced. "That was my twenty-year-old ego talking. When you decided to not go with me, I just... I was mad, and I missed the hell out of you, okay? I admit that I didn't handle it well."

After they'd graduated high school, they'd moved in together and both gone to the local community college. Their plan was to transfer to the state school their junior year. But then Lucas had gotten an academic scholarship to a small private school back East. One that was way too expensive for Hope to manage without crippling debt. So even though he'd asked her to go with him, she'd declined and stayed in Premonition Pointe, thinking they'd do long distance for two years and then he'd come home.

"Can you just tell me the truth about something?" she asked, already feeling defeated. She didn't want to have this argument again, but here they were over twenty years later, still hashing out their past.

"Of course. I've never lied to you."

She stared into his unrelenting gaze and decided that he was telling the truth. But she still had to ask. "Did you break it off back then because you'd met someone?"

Lucas sucked in a deep breath, and Hope felt like her heart was going to bust in two. How could she still not be over something that happened twenty-six years ago? It was because it was Lucas, and she'd never gotten over him. "Yes and no."

Hope rolled her eyes. "That isn't an answer."

"I know. Here's the truth. I did meet someone. She asked me out, and I was so lonely that I wanted to go. You and I, we were everything to each other. And at the time, you were working and going to school full-time. Our schedules were completely out of sync, and I just needed someone in my life. So I told you that maybe it was better if we allowed each other to see other people while I was at school."

"And I flipped out," Hope said, still feeling the echo of the pain she'd felt back then.

"Yeah. I tried to take it back, but it was too late. You told me to live my life and you'd live yours. And if I ever came home again, not to count on your being available." He let out a low chuckle. "Dammit, Hope. You were so hardheaded back then. I expected you to find someone and marry them right away just to spite me."

She had considered it. But she'd never fallen in love with anyone else. Besides, getting married had never been her style anyway. "And the girl you wanted to date? How'd that work out for you?"

"We didn't date. We went to dinner one night and became really good friends. That's it," he said.

"That's it? Really? You didn't sleep with her?"

He shook his head. "Hope, I didn't sleep with anyone but you while I was in school."

"You're kidding?" she asked, shocked. "Seriously?"

"Do you really think I'd lie to you, especially now that I know you can read my thoughts?" he asked with a chuckle.

"I'm not reading your thoughts," she said. "In fact, I'm actively trying to not invade your privacy."

He tightened his hold on her hand and shook his head slightly, looking amused. "That right there is one of the reasons I never got over you."

"Why's that? Because I have some ethics?" Because if that was the reason, he was giving her far too much credit considering she'd just spent half the week trying to listen in on the residents of the town.

"Because you have a good heart and you always want to do the right thing. You love passionately and are fiercely protective of those you love. I miss that. I miss you."

She desperately wanted to avert her gaze again, but she didn't. It seemed important that she tell him her truth. "I miss you, too."

Relief flooded his eyes, and his shoulders seemed to relax slightly. "You obviously know I've been hoping to rekindle what we had. You had to know it the moment you realized I bought our house."

She just nodded because refusing to acknowledge what was between them was futile. At some point, they both needed to decide if they were going to try again or walk away for good. Because they couldn't keep dancing around each other forever.

"Do you think we can try this out? See where it goes?" he asked.

The waitress appeared, interrupting them to take their order. Hope ordered the linguine with clams while Lucas went with the scallops. After their server left, Hope took a sip of wine, stalling for time.

Lucas sat back in his chair and waited. His gaze was fixated on her, as if he were the one trying to read her mind now.

Finally, she said, "I just don't know. I want to say yes, but I just don't trust you to not leave again."

There is was. The undeniable truth that kept tearing them apart. Twice now, she'd given herself to him completely and he'd left. How could she go through that again?

"I don't plan to leave again," he said.

"You didn't the last two times either," she countered.

He leaned forward. "Can I ask *you* something?"

"Sure." She didn't have anything to hide. But if he started asking her about the men she'd dated, it was going to quickly get very uncomfortable.

"Why wasn't I important enough for you to take a chance on leaving this town? I asked you both times to come with me."

Asked was a mild way of putting it. He'd actually begged her to go with him the second time. Lucas had been offered a prestigious apprenticeship with a world-renowned woodworker. There was no doubt that the reason he was so successful now was because of that education and the business contacts he'd made. "You were important. You *are* important. But so was I. First I had to get my education." Hope had a business degree with an emphasis on marketing. It had served her well. "Then when you got your apprenticeship, I'd just open my art gallery. Not only did I have a bunch of artists relying on me, but it was starting to take off. How could I just give that up to follow a man around the country?"

"A man?" he asked, frowning. "So, I'm just a man now?"

"No. But look at it from my perspective. If you had just opened your retail shop and it was taking off, and I asked you to move for my education with no plan for what you were going to do, would you have done it?"

Silence.

"That's what I thought." She picked up another piece of bread and slathered it generously with butter. Normally she tried to keep her bread intake to just one piece so she wouldn't be too full for her meal, but this conversation was driving her to OD on the carbs. Didn't he understand that she needed to be her own person? That she couldn't and wouldn't just drop all of her dreams for someone else?

"I think I would have done it for you," he finally said.

Hope dropped the roll onto a small plate. "Seriously? If I told you right now that I was taking a job in Denver or Chicago, you'd close your shop and just come with me?"

"If we could work it out so my mom could come with us and have good care, yes, I would."

She narrowed her eyes at him. "But you didn't stay before."

"I know. Life is different now."

"How is it different?" she asked, exasperated. Why was he making it sound like she was the selfish one? She'd never run away from him. In fact, she'd stayed put in Premonition Pointe her entire life. If he'd been so desperate to be with her, he knew where to find her.

"I've realized what's most important. When I was

younger, I had something to prove. Now…" He shrugged. "I just want to live a life that makes me happy. You always made me happy."

But for how long, she couldn't help but think to herself. How long until something better came along and he wanted her to uproot her life for him? "I just don't know, Lucas. You know that I've always loved you. But it's been a long time since we've been together, and it took way too long for me to get over you the second time. I just don't know if this is a good idea for either of us."

"It's a good idea, Hope. In fact, I guarantee that it's the best idea I've ever had. I'm definitely not going anywhere. And I'll spend the rest of my days here on earth proving that to you. All I'm asking is that you think about it, to consider dating me again. I'm not asking for forever tonight. But I'll warn you; it *is* my end goal."

Dammit. Why was he sitting across from her saying all the things she'd wanted to hear fifteen years ago? She desperately wanted to say yes, but the word just wouldn't pass her lips. Her eyes stung with unshed tears as she said, "I just need some time."

"Time is something I have in abundance. Take all you need, and when you're ready, I'll be here waiting to sweep you off your feet."

That was just it. She didn't want to be swept off her feet. She wanted stability. Consistency. Trust. Could she find that with Lucas? Or would he always be knocking her off her axis?

CHAPTER FOURTEEN

"*H*ow about a walk on the beach?" Lucas asked when he was driving her home from Abalone.

She glanced out the window at the gigantic full moon and the light reflecting off the ocean. It was one of those rare perfect evenings when the winds had died down and time seemed to stand still. "I'd love a walk on the beach."

He pulled his truck into a parking lot at the public access and then ran around to her door to open it for her.

"Thank you," she said, letting him help her down.

"You're very welcome." He slipped his hand into hers, and when they got to the sand, they both kicked off their shoes and continued on toward the water.

"Remember that time we came down here and watched those people skinny-dipping?" Lucas asked out of the blue.

She glanced at him and started laughing. "The old people you mean?"

"They weren't old. Late thirties. Early forties at the most."

"Yeah, that's old to eighteen-year-olds," she said. Then she added, "Why were you thinking about that?"

"Well… It's a really nice night. If you were interested, I could probably be talked into it." He had a cheeky grin that made her shake her head.

"You want me to get naked and dive into the Pacific Ocean? The *freezing* Pacific Ocean? Have you lost your mind?"

"No." He stopped and stared out at the sea. "I just remember how much fun they were having. They were laughing and playing and seemed to really be in the moment. It's been a long while since I've felt that way, and I thought… Well, I really wanted to experience that with you."

Oh, hell. Hope's heart started to pound against her breastbone as she studied his profile. She could see his long eyelashes in the moonlight, and something shifted inside of her. The resistance she'd been holding onto so tightly eased, and she could no longer deny herself the one thing she'd always wanted. To be connected to Lucas again.

"It would be pretty bold to take it all off right here don't you think?" she asked him.

His gaze shifted to hers, and a slow smile tilted his lips. "What do you think? Should we move to the cove?"

"If we want to hold onto a shred of our dignity, it's probably a good idea. I mean, considering we both have businesses in town, we should probably—"

"Let's go." He grabbed her hand and started running down the beach.

Hope let out a yelp but quickly matched his pace, and by the time they rounded the large rocky outcropping into a protected cove, she was gasping for breath from laughing too hard.

Lucas stripped off his blazer and then grabbed the bottom of his T-shirt. "I'm ready when you're ready."

She stopped laughing and stared at him, willing him to lose his shirt. How long had It been since she'd seen his chest and eight-pack abs? Did he even have an eight pack anymore?

"Hey, Anderson. Eyes up here." He used two fingers to point toward his face.

"Please. Like the minute I start de-robing you aren't going to be staring?" she asked.

"Fair enough. But I know how you operate, and I'm not going to be the only one who gets naked. Either we do this together, or we're calling it off."

She threw her head back and laughed. It would be just like her to pretend she was going to join him and then bail at the last minute while he dove into the chilly water.

"See. I knew it." He grabbed her hand and pulled her forward until she was pressed against his chest. His rock-hard chest. She leaned into him, soaking up the warmth radiating from him. "Are you all-in on this, Hope? Can I trust you?"

For a moment, she wasn't sure if he was talking about skinny-dipping or their relationship. But then he added, "Because I'm not getting naked unless you do."

She patted his chest and smiled up at him. "I'm in. On three?"

He nodded and took a step back. "On three."

She counted backward, and when she got to one, she shrugged out of her sweater and started untying her wrap dress.

"Damn, you're really doing this," he said, his voice husky.

Hope paused. "Only if you start showing some skin."

Grinning, he reached behind his shoulder and grabbed the back of his shirt to pull it over his head. Hope's breath caught in her throat. How was it possible that he was even more beautiful than she remembered?

His hands paused on his belt buckle. "Are you still with me?"

"Uh-huh." She quickly shrugged out of her dress, leaving her standing in her bra and panties.

It was Lucas's turn to stare.

"I think you might be drooling," she said.

"No doubt." He made a show of wiping his mouth with the back of his hand, and then he quickly climbed out of his jeans, leaving them both in their underwear.

"Are we going in like this, or are we going the full monty?" she asked.

"It wouldn't be skinny-dipping if we're still covered," he said with a challenge in his voice.

"No, it would not." Without hesitation, she unhooked her bra and dropped it onto her dress.

"Holy mother of sin," he whispered as his gaze locked onto her chest. He took a step forward, reaching for her, but Hope stepped back out of his reach.

"Nope. We're going in that water. And if you start that, we both know what will happen."

"I'm definitely okay with that." His voice was strained as if he was barely holding himself back.

Hope was in full agreement with him, but she still had enough wits about her that she wasn't going to get down and dirty right there on a public beach. Skinny-dipping was one thing. But rolling around in the sand, getting it in places it was never meant to be, was not on the table. Besides, if someone did happen to see them skinny-dipping, it would be a funny story. Fornicating in public was an entirely different matter.

"That's not going to happen. But if you drop your drawers, I might let you cop a feel once we're in the water." She shimmied out of her lace panties.

Lucas yanked his boxer briefs off, and after grabbing her hand again, they both ran full speed into the icy water.

"Oh, holy shit!" Hope screamed when Lucas pulled her into the surf, dunking both of them. She quickly popped up, gasping and shivering from the ocean water.

"Damn, that's a lot colder than I remembered," Lucas said in her ear as he wrapped his arms around her, his hands cupping her breasts.

With his hard body pressed up against the back of hers, suddenly she didn't care about the cold. All she wanted was to stand there in the water with him wrapped around her forever.

"Are you okay?" he whispered.

"Yeah." She nodded and leaned her head against his shoulder as she covered his hands with her own. "I'm more than okay. I might even be perfect."

He let out a low growl and bent his head to trail kisses down her neck. A shiver that didn't have anything to do with the cold rippled through her. And before she could think better of it, she turned and wrapped her arms around his neck and kissed him with everything she had.

His mouth opened for hers, and she let herself get lost in him. He tasted of a hint of chocolate and coffee, and of love and home. She slid one hand into his wet hair and moved the other one down to slide it over his bare—

"Ahh!" A wave hit them and knocked them both over into the surf again, breaking the magic.

"Ohmigod, it's too damned cold in here." Her teeth

started chattering, and without a word, Lucas picked her up and carried her back to the beach.

Once they reached their clothes, he set her back on her feet and started running his hands up and down her arms to try to warm her up.

"Are you all right?" he asked.

She nodded, her teeth still chattering as she fumbled with putting her underwear back on. "We really should've considered towels."

"That would've killed the spontaneity," he said, giving her a wide smile.

"It would've saved us from having to put our clothes on while dripping wet," she groused.

"Here." He handed her his Nirvana T-shirt. "Use this to dry off."

She took the shirt but didn't use it. "You're going to freeze without this."

"I have my blazer. Dry off so you can get back into your dress." He stepped closer and kissed her gently on the forehead. "I promise; I'm fine."

She gave him a grateful smile and dried herself off and handed the T-shirt back to him. He did the same, and they both quickly got dressed. Hope wrapped her sweater around herself and let out a sigh of relief. "That is so much better."

Dressed in his jeans and blazer, Lucas balled his wet shirt up in one hand and draped his arm over Hope's shoulder as they walked back to his truck.

"Thank you for this," she said, leaning into him to soak up his warmth.

"No need to thank me. I'd do this every day of the week if you were game."

She laughed. "Maybe next time we try a hot tub."

"There's going to be a next time?" he asked hopefully.

"Yeah," she said softly. "There's definitely going to be a next time."

Lucas stopped suddenly, spun her around, and pressed his lips to hers. The kiss was possessive and full of fire and over far too quickly, leaving her breathless. Lucas pulled back slightly and said, "I wanted to seal that with a kiss."

She smiled up at him, completely charmed and slightly overwhelmed. This was why she always found her way back to him.

The thought slammed into her and made her step back to put space between them. She cleared her throat. "We should probably get going."

He stared at her for a long moment and then nodded. "You're probably right." He held his hand out to her, and even though she hesitated, she still wrapped her fingers around his and let him lead her back to the truck.

The ride to her house was only a few minutes, but the silence between them made it feel like forever. When he finally pulled up in front of her house, she was ready to jump out and run inside. But he killed the engine, and as he always did, he opened her door and walked her up to the front porch.

"I had a really wonderful time tonight," he said.

"So did I." She chuckled to herself. "I can't believe we went skinny-dipping."

"I can." He brushed her wet hair back and asked, "When can I see you again?"

Hope wanted to say tomorrow night. But something niggled at her that maybe she had plans. Was that with Grace or Joy? She couldn't quite remember. So she said, "How about Sunday brunch? We could meet at that farm-to-table place. Blueberries?"

"Sounds perfect. But I'll pick you up at ten." Before she could answer, he pulled her into him again and brushed his lips over hers in a soft, sweet kiss as his hands roamed down her back and squeezed her butt.

Hope melted into him, and if her mother hadn't been inside, she was certain she'd have opened the door and tugged him straight to her bedroom.

Lucas let her go and stepped back. "Goodnight, Hope."

She brought her fingertips to her lips and whispered, "Goodnight."

She stood on her porch with her hand on the knob and waited for him to get into his truck before she finally went inside and closed the door gently behind her.

"Looks like someone had a good evening," Angela said from her spot where she was curled up on the couch.

"I did. But I don't know if that's a good thing."

"You can't keep running from him forever, bunny."

Hope gave her mother a curious look. "Why? I don't see you tied to anyone."

Her mother's expression turned sad as she shook her head. "You're right. It's not in the cards for me. I need too much space to make a relationship work, but anyone with eyes can see you and Lucas belong together. If you both hadn't been so stubborn, you'd have already worked out a way to be together."

"You really don't think there's a quiet man or woman out there for you?" Hope asked, her heart aching for her mom. Hope had been so focused on her own feelings of abandonment that she hadn't taken the time to really understand what the curse had meant for her mom.

She shrugged. "I've dated some. I'm better off alone. At seventy-four, I'm not about to change my ways now. It would be very hard for me to make room for a partner in my life." Angela got to her feet and moved to her daughter. She pressed a kiss to her cheek and said, "I'm glad you enjoyed yourself. I'm headed to bed."

"Thanks. Goodnight, Mom."

Angela moved past her down the hall. Just before she slipped into her bedroom, she added, "Next time, try the beach on the north side of town. You'll have more privacy."

CHAPTER FIFTEEN

$\mathcal{H}$ope woke to the sun streaming over her face. She rubbed the sleep out of her eyes and groaned when she saw that is was past ten. Her thoughts were cloudy from sleeping too long, and her head was aching from the lack of caffeine.

After rolling out of bed and wrapping herself in her terry cloth robe, she shuffled into the kitchen, desperate for coffee.

"Morning, bunny." Her mom was fully dressed and sat at the table with her feet propped up on one of the other chairs, sipping from a mug.

"Morning," she mumbled, fully focused on her mission for caffeine.

"I ran into Maggie Peters this morning while I was at the Pointe of View Café listening in on people. She said she booked you for a wedding shower next month," Angela said.

"Yeah. That's right. Her daughter's getting married in October." Hope poured the last of the coffee into her mug and took a long sip before going to work on making a fresh pot. One cup wasn't going to cut it.

"She wanted me to give you a message."

Hope glanced up at her mother. "What's that? Did she want to change the venue again?"

Angela shook her head. "No. Actually she said she needed to cancel. Something about a scheduling conflict."

"Cancel? What?" Why the heck was one of her clients telling her mother they wanted to cancel? Why hadn't Maggie just called so they could work something out?

"She told me there was a scheduling conflict, but I think it's really something else." Angela handed her a blueberry muffin from the bakery takeout box on the table.

Hope took it and waited for her mother to continue.

"As we were standing there, I heard her thinking about someone named Peggy and how grateful she was for the heads up."

"Heads up about what?" Peggy Pitsman was Hope's competition. What exactly had she told Maggie?

"I have no idea. Do you know Peggy?"

Hope nodded. "She just started doing events. Mostly showers and birthday parties."

Angela's eyes narrowed. "Is she sabotaging your business?"

It sure sounded like it. "I don't know, but I'll call Maggie and find out what's going on… after coffee." Hope started to move back toward her bedroom, hoping that a shower would help her aching head. But just before she left the kitchen she glanced back at her mother. "Thanks, Mom."

Angela's expression brightened as she smiled warmly at her daughter. "You're welcome."

* * *

AFTER A SHOWER and some pain killers, Hope settled into her home office and gave Maggie a call. It went straight to voicemail.

"Great," she muttered and then left a message asking her to call as soon as possible to work out the cancelation details. Then she went to work on pulling together some possibilities for Skyler's dog wedding event. She spent a fair amount of time on the internet, checking trends and making a bunch of notes, and then she checked out a barkery website to see what kind of treats might be appropriate for a canine wedding. After she printed out pictures of different options, she moved on to checking the details of a grand opening for a handmade glass gallery. The event was a couple weeks out, and Hope still hadn't gotten an answer on if Yasmeen wanted to offer the mini cheesecakes or the mini cupcakes. She was going to need to let the bakery know soon.

She once again grabbed her phone.

"Oh, Hope. It's good you called," Yasmeen said by way of greeting.

"Good morning, or should I say afternoon?" Hope asked, eyeing her wall clock. It was just after noon, and the day was slipping away from her.

"Um... listen," Yasmeen said hesitantly. "I think it's best if we cancel the plans for the grand opening."

"What happened? Do you have to move the date?" Hope asked.

"No. It's not that. I've just decided that something lower key is probably better for us."

Hope was momentarily stunned. Lower key? What did that mean? Hope had been planning something similar to what she'd done with Lucas's open house, which meant some food and drinks, a couple of artists doing demonstrations, and plenty of press. "If it's a matter of my fees, we can work something out—"

"It's not that," she said quickly and then sighed heavily. "Listen, Hope, I don't really have a lot of time right now. I know I'm forfeiting my deposit. Let's just leave it there."

"Yeah, okay. I'm sorry it didn't work out," Hope said.

"So am I." Yasmeen ended the call, and Hope tossed her phone onto her desk and tried to process what just happened. Two cancelations in one day? It was rare for her to have *one* client cancel, and when they did, usually they just rescheduled rather than canceling all together.

Hope opened her email and immediately found one from the town's senior fundraising group. The subject line said, *Need to Cancel.* Hope's heart started to race. She clicked on the email and ground her teeth. The event to raise money for the town bike path was supposed to be a casino night that they'd asked Hope to coordinate. Apparently, the event was still on, but Hope's involvement was no longer needed. Norma, the president of the group, hadn't said why, only that if Hope had incurred any expenses so far that she should submit them to their group's accountant.

"This is ridiculous!" Hope cried, jumping out of her chair. Something was going on, and she needed to get to the bottom of it. She tried calling Maggie again, and when that was unsuccessful, she tried the president of the fundraising group. Again, the phone went unanswered.

Pacing, Hope decided she had two choices. She could confront Peggy Pitsman or find Maggie or Norma and get some answers. Since Yasmeen hadn't been forthcoming when they spoke, Hope decided she was a lost cause for now. She didn't know where to find Norma since her group only met twice a month at the library. But Maggie owned a bike shop not far from the square.

After grabbing her keys, Hope stormed out of her house and drove to the middle of town. It was a gorgeous day with clear blue skies and a light breeze that blew in off the ocean. It seemed as if the entire population of Premonition Pointe was out enjoying the fall day. But it was all lost on Hope. She was single-focused. Her business was suddenly on fire, and she needed to put it out.

Parking near the square proved impossible, so Hope chose a spot a few blocks away in front of Lucas's store. She was so determined to find Maggie that she barely even glanced in his shop. She made out the shape of a couple of people and assumed he was working with a customer. There was no time to say hello anyway.

Hope walked so fast she was nearly out of breath when she finally found Maggie's bike shop. She rounded the half dozen bikes that were lined up outside and ducked into the store.

A young man who couldn't have been older than twenty looked up from where he was assembling a bike. "Can I help you?"

"Is Maggie in?" Hope asked, craning her neck to get a glimpse in the back.

"Nope. She's out to lunch. She should be back in thirty minutes or so. Did you want to leave your number?"

"No. I'll come back. Thanks." Hope didn't trust that Maggie would get in touch with her. Not after the way she'd canceled by giving her mother the message. Hope stepped back outside and scanned the area for somewhere to sit so that she could see Maggie when she returned. But as she eyed the area, Maggie's bright red curls stood out in the park where she sat at a picnic table.

Hope straightened her shoulders and made her way across the square to the grassy area, and without asking to be invited, she sat down opposite Maggie and said, "Hello."

Maggie jerked her head up, clearly startled, and that's when Hope noticed the ear buds jammed in her ears. The woman tugged them out and said, "Hope. What are you doing here?"

"I was just running some errands and spotted you here. Thought I'd say hi. I'm not interrupting your lunch, am I?" Hope nodded to the half-eaten burger sitting in front of her.

"Well, actually I was just reading a little before I went back to work." Her apologetic expression made it clear she expected Hope to move on, but that wasn't going to happen.

Hope ignored the implication and leaned forward. "Listen, I heard you ran into my mother this morning at the café."

"Yeah, about that... I, uh..." Her face flushed and she glanced away. *What is she doing here?* Maggie thought so loudly that it almost made Hope wince.

Hope followed her gaze and spotted a man with a mic who was standing in front of the new dog park and appeared to be delivering a segment for the local news station. "Hey, no worries. She said you had a scheduling conflict, so I was thinking we can just move the date. I'm sure I can make it work. I just need the details."

"I don't think that's a good idea." Maggie got up and tossed her burger into a nearby garbage can. Then she thought, *I don't need to explain myself to your type.*

'Your type'? What the hell did that mean? "Oh? Was there a problem with my work?"

"No." Her tone was clipped now. "I just changed my mind, okay? Do I have to have a reason?"

"If it has anything to do with Peggy Pitsman you do," Hope challenged, no longer trying to be nice about whatever was happening. Her business was on the line, and she had to get to the bottom of things.

"All Peggy did was warn me about what happened at your last event. And I can't take that risk, so let's just leave it at that."

Her last event? That was Lucas's open house. Maggie started to walk away, but Hope reached out and grabbed her wrist, stopping her. "What do you mean? Nothing unusual happened at Against the Grain."

Maggie stared at Hope's hand and said, "Let go of me."

Hope dropped her wrist instantly. "Sorry. I'm just trying to understand. Lucas's event was a success."

Maggie snorted derisively. "Yeah. *I heard.*"

Now Hope was just getting pissed. "Heard *what* exactly?"

"Oh, come on, Hope. You're not going to make me say it, are you?"

"Say what?" Hope threw her hands up, completely over this conversation that appeared to be going nowhere fast. "Just spit it out, okay? I'm completely lost."

"The fact that this is just an everyday occurrence for you, like it's normal, is what makes it worse," Maggie hissed. "I never would've thought you'd be trading sexual favors to get ahead."

"What?" Hope jerked back like she'd been struck and stared at the woman in complete shock. "Sexual favors? What the hell did Peggy tell you?"

"This isn't the place, Hope. If I were you, I'd back away."

"No. I'm not going anywhere until you tell me what

145

Peggy told you." Hope placed her hands on her hips, determined to get to the bottom of whatever she was talking about. "Who exactly did I supposedly sleep with to get a job?"

Chatter rose up around her, but Hope was too laser focused on Maggie to pay much attention.

"Well, Lucas for one. Everyone knows what you two got up to last night. It's all over town. And there have been rumors about others. Why else would Pauly Pitsman have you plan his annual holiday party instead of his niece?" she asked. Then Maggie's thoughts came through loud and clear. *I bet you showed the man the time of his life to spend that kind of money.*

Maybe he didn't hire Peggy because Pauly's niece had no idea how to put together the elegant event he planned every year for all of his business contacts. But she didn't say that. There was zero basis to that claim. Instead, she blurted, "All Lucas and I did was take a dip in the ocean. There's nothing wrong with that. No sexual favors were traded for anything."

"You were naked!" Maggie cried. "You expect me to believe it was innocent?"

"So what? We went skinny-dipping. Who hasn't in this town?" Hope cried.

The chatter around her diminished, and Hope finally tore her gaze from Maggie to see the news guy who'd been doing a segment over by the dog park was standing right beside her.

He quickly shoved the mic in her face. "Ms. Anderson, do you care to respond to the allegation of trading sexual favors for contracts?"

Hope's entire body went numb as she processed what was happening.

"She doesn't need to," Maggie stated. Her arms were

crossed over her chest, and she was scowling so fiercely that she looked like a schoolteacher who'd just caught Hope and Lucas making out in the eraser closet. "She's already confirmed inappropriate behavior with Lucas King, the owner of Against the Grain Interiors. I'm sure if you do some digging, you'll find out that all of her current clients are canceling their agreements with her. No one wants to be associated with her kind."

The news guy nodded and turned to speak into the camera. "And there you have it, folks. Hope Anderson's event planning business appears to be on the rocks. Morals and decency have once again won the day here in Premonition Pointe."

CHAPTER SIXTEEN

*H*ope was fuming. She was so angry she couldn't even talk. Words just sputtered out of her mouth incoherently as she watched the reporter retreat back to his news van. After he'd made his incredibly biased statement on camera, she given him a piece of her mind, but it was too late. The segment was over, and the entire town would now think she was sleeping around to secure jobs. And to make matters worse, most of her male clients were married.

Just perfect. She'd be labeled an adulteress. Hope bet that if she walked around the square she'd hear all kinds of unsavory thoughts about herself. She grimaced and decided her best course of action was to go home and write a press release addressing the newscast and hope that her past clients would deny the nefarious rumors.

Hope spun around and immediately crashed into the solid form of a half-naked man. "Oomph."

"Whoa there, gorgeous."

She tried to step back but found herself encircled in very familiar arms. She knew those arms. And they weren't the

149

ones she wanted holding her. Hope pressed her palm to Benji's chest and gently pushed him back. "Hey. What are you doing here?"

He raised one eyebrow. "I thought I had a hot date tonight."

Son of a… She'd completely forgotten that she'd made the date with her casual hookup. But that still didn't explain why he was in the square half naked. "No, I mean why are you *here*? And where are your clothes?"

Benji brushed his dark curls out of his eyes and laughed. "I decided to get some surfing in this morning. The waves were killer until the wind died down. Then I thought I'd grab some lunch before going back to my hotel. Imagine my surprise when I saw you talking with that soccer mom and then heard you say you'd gone skinny-dipping last night. And now I want to know why we've never splashed around in the ocean in our birthday suits." His lips were curled into a sexy little smile, and he was looking at her like he wanted to devour her right there. "Wanna try for a repeat tonight?"

She couldn't do this. Not after her night with Lucas the night before and not after she'd found out Peggy Pitsman was trying to sabotage her business. Hope started to shake her head, intending to decline his invitation and then find a graceful way to back out of the date, but she was interrupted when she heard another familiar male voice say, "Hope's busy tonight."

"Lucas?" she spun around again and found him standing with his fists clenched at his side and glaring at Benji. If her life hadn't felt like it was imploding, she might have appreciated the scene. Benji was tanned and fit in his board shorts and looked adorable with his messy curls hanging over one eye, while Lucas was dressed in jeans, a white T-shirt, and a navy blazer. He looked every bit a successful, stylish business owner. Damn, they were both hot. But she only wanted one of them.

"Who is this guy, Hope?" Lucas asked, staring at her intently.

"Whoa, man. Chill. I'm just a friend," Benji said, and Hope could've kissed him for not mentioning that they were friends with benefits.

"Sounds like something more than friends," Lucas said, running one hand through his salt and pepper hair.

"Well, friends can have fun every once in a while, right babe?" Benji said, winking at Hope.

Hope groaned and turned to Lucas. "Can you give us a minute? Then I'll fill you in?"

He stared down at her, his jaw clenched and his eyes full of... anger? Frustration? Hurt? She wasn't quite sure. But the reality was that he didn't have any right to be angry with her. They'd had one date and hadn't talked about making any commitments. She was still free to date whomever she wanted, right? Just because they'd kissed the night before didn't mean anything.

Liar, she thought to herself. She just wasn't willing to voice what was really happening between them.

Lucas put his hands up and walked away.

"What's that guy's problem?" Benji asked, placing a hand on the back of her neck. Normally she would've leaned into a touch like that. But instead, she stepped away from him, feeling like he was trying to claim her or something.

"That's my ex," she said.

Benji's gaze flickered over to where Lucas was sitting on a bench, staring at them. "Which one?"

Hope had a number of exes. Most of them she'd only

dated for a short time and then they'd become friends. In fact, two of them had made her the godmother of their children. Both had moved to the city, so she didn't see them often, but she sent cards and gifts to their kids, so she didn't completely disappear out of their lives. Lucas was pretty much the only ex she'd severed contact with after their breakup. It had just been too painful. "*The* ex. The reason why this"—she moved her hand between the two of them —"has never been more than casual."

"*The* ex?" he echoed. "Oh. Interesting." He smiled down at her, and the thoughts came spilling out of his head. *I bet I can make her forget him. I just need a few minutes and somewhere private.*

"It's going to take more than a few minutes."

"Um, what?" he asked, chuckling. "Did I say that out loud?"

Dammit! He hadn't, had he? Instead of acknowledging his question, she said, "Listen, Benji, I'm really sorry about this, but I need to cancel. Last night with Lucas was... Well, I don't know what it was, but now I just feel like it's not right to go out with someone else. Not until I figure out how I feel about him walking back into my life."

He stepped closer to her and pressed his palm to her cheek, running his thumb over her cheekbone. Normally her skin tingled when he touched her like that. But now her skin felt tight, maybe even itchy, and all she wanted to do was step back and reclaim her space. She stayed put, though, letting him have his say. "You know I'm the better man for you, right?"

Hope let out a surprised bark of laughter. "Is that so? How?"

"I'm easy. I make you feel good. And there are no

expectations. No drama. Just a good time. I can make you forget him. You know I can."

There was a time when all of that was true, but things had changed. "You've always been a good friend, Benji. I'm sorry to stand you up. Will you forgive me?"

He glanced over at Lucas one more time and back at her. "It's like that then? You're going to go for it?"

She shrugged. "To tell you the truth, I don't have any clue what I'm doing, but I do know that going out with you tonight isn't fair to any of us. Especially you, because I'll really want to be with him."

"It sounds like you've already made your decision."

"I guess so. I'm sorry you drove up here and wasted money on a hotel." She shoved her hands into the pockets of her jeans.

"Don't worry about me. The surfing makes it all worthwhile. And I'm sure I can get into some trouble at the bar tonight."

She laughed. "I'm sure you can."

"Do me one favor?" he asked.

"What's that?"

"Call me if it doesn't work out." He leaned down and brushed a kiss over her cheek and then strode off across the square.

Hope watched him go, and when she finally resolved her nerve, she turned back toward Lucas and found an empty bench instead. Dread formed in the pit of her stomach as she glanced around, looking for him. When it was evident that he'd left, she blew out a breath and started to make her way back toward Against the Grain.

CHAPTER SEVENTEEN

"What do you mean he just left?" Grace asked as she poured a glass of iced tea for Hope.

"I mean that he was there one moment, and as soon as Benji left, he disappeared," Hope said, exasperated. "I even went back to his store, but the door was locked and the sign said *Closed*. And he's not answering my phone calls."

Grace grabbed the two glasses of tea and jerked her head toward her living room. "Let's sit in there. It's comfier than those dining room chairs."

Hope followed her friend and flopped onto her overstuffed couch, wondering how she'd managed to get so entangled with Lucas so quickly. Hadn't she told herself she wasn't going to do that again?

"Want me to call him?" Grace asked, sitting with her legs crossed and facing Hope on the couch. "Track him down so you can tell him… whatever it is you need to tell him?"

"Gods, no." Hope gave her a look indicating she thought her friend was crazy. "What am I? A thirteen-year-old?"

Grace chuckled and grinned at her friend. "If the shoe fits."

"Shut it, Valentine. I seem to recall it wasn't all that long ago when you were angsting about a certain younger guy. And who was here to help you figure that out?"

"You were. Thank you for that by the way. He's... just what I needed," Grace said.

Hope snorted. "I bet."

It felt good to be at Grace's house, even if the reason Hope had barged in on her friend was because she was having a meltdown about the men in her life. Or, more specifically, one man in her life.

"Okay, so tell me again what happened. He was there one minute and not the next, right? What happened in that minute?" Grace asked.

"I don't know. I was just talking to Benji, breaking our date that I'd forgotten all about, actually, and then after Benji left, I realized Lucas had bailed, too," Hope said, clutching her iced tea.

"Did you hug Benji goodbye or touch him or anything?" Grace asked, her brows furrowed.

"No. I didn't, but... Oh, crap." Hope closed her eyes and slumped back into the couch. "Benji touched me. He caressed my cheek and then kissed me goodbye."

"He kissed you! And you're wondering why Lucas bolted?" The incredulity in her voice made Hope cringe.

"He kissed me on the cheek. It's not like I made out with the guy," Hope insisted. "Jeez. Was that really enough to send him running? After everything that's gone down, that's going to be the final straw?"

"Hope," Grace said, shaking her head. "Seriously? You just told me that your date with him was magical. That you guys told each other that you'd try again. And then the very next day, he finds out you have a date with your booty call and watches the guy kiss you. Wouldn't that send you running? How would you feel if you saw him with some other chick that he'd obviously been banging before you came back into his life?"

"That's…" Hope groaned. She'd been about to deny that she'd be upset if the situation were reversed, but that would be a blatant lie. She'd have bolted, too. It was even likely she'd call off whatever it was they were doing. "This is really a mess. I should've canceled earlier, but I completely forgot about it."

"Love does that to a person," Grace said.

"Don't say that word." Hope buried her face in her hands. When she finally came up for air, she said, "There's something else."

"Really?" Grace asked, surprised.

Before Hope could continue, the door swung open and in walked Lex, Grace's niece.

"Hey!" She held a bag of groceries in one hand and waved with the other. "What are you two up to? Looks like gossip."

"It is," Grace said. "Put those groceries away and come join us. Hope can tell you all about her love triangle."

"I don't have a love triangle," Hope insisted, rolling her eyes.

"Well, not anymore," Grace said with a chuckle.

Hope glanced at where Lex had disappeared into the kitchen. "Why is Lex doing your grocery shopping? I thought she moved in with her girlfriend."

"She did. She's here to help me make dinner. Owen is coming over, and I told him I'd cook."

Hope laughed. "So, Lex is saving you so it will be edible?"

"That I am," Lex said as she strode back into the room and sat next to Hope, wrapping an arm around her shoulders. "I heard some crazy stuff about you today."

Hope sighed. "How bad is it?"

"Bad enough that the entire town is talking about it," Lex said with a grimace. "You didn't really have sex with Pauly Pitsman just to organize his elaborate Christmas party every year, did you?"

"Wait. What?" Grace exclaimed as she sat up.

"Of course not," Hope said and then launched into and explanation, starting with her clients canceling and then ending with what happened at the square with Maggie and the reporter. "I know this is all on Peggy Pitsman. Does she really think that everyone is going to believe this garbage?"

"Maybe," Grace said. "You did confirm on camera that you went skinny-dipping with Lucas, who is one of your clients."

"But Pauly Pitsman? And other people in town? Come on!" Hope cried. "Everyone knows that Lucas and I dated off and on in the past. Us getting back together isn't all that shocking."

"Of course it isn't." Grace patted her knee. "But think about it. There are a lot of new people in town since you and Lucas were together last time. Not everyone knows your story. And you have been a serial dater. They aren't used to seeing you with one man."

"None of that means she's a whore, Aunt Grace," Lex admonished, clearly frustrated on Hope's behalf.

"I know that, honey. I was just painting the scenario of what some of the busybodies in town are going to latch onto in order to make Hope's life miserable. We need to get in front of this. The sooner the better," Grace said.

"I agree, but other than putting out a press release that probably no one will read, I'm not sure how to go about that," Hope said.

"Leave it to me." Lex popped up off the couch.

"What are you going to do?" Hope eyed her with suspicion.

"Don't worry about it. I've got this. You just worry about Lucas and how you're going to fix the mess you're in." She leaned down and hugged Hope.

They watched as Lex made her way back to the kitchen.

"What do you think she's up to?" Hope asked Grace.

"I bet she puts her circle to work on exposing Peggy Pitsman," Grace said. "Peggy was the mean mom when Lex was in school. She was the president of the PTA before she decided to be an event planner. Anyway, she was always trying to make sure her daughter was at the center of everything, even if it meant taking opportunities away from other kids. My bet is that Lex and Jackson would just love a reason to put her in her place."

As lovely as that sounded, Hope didn't want the situation to get any worse. She got up and joined Lex at the kitchen counter. "Hey, I just wanted to make sure we're on the same page about this accusation that's been lobbed at me."

"Okay. Shoot." Lex, who was a trained chef, was already busy chopping vegetables for the dinner she was making for Grace and Owen.

"You're not going to do anything crazy, are you? Like try to get revenge on Peggy Pitsman for being a total raging bitch?"

Lex let out a bark of laughter. "Are you saying you don't want to see Peggy go down in flames?"

"No. I'd love to see that. I just don't want the situation to get worse. I can't help but imagine both of us ending up on a daytime talk show explaining how we were both arrested for having a cat fight over something stupid like the last helium tank at the party supply store."

Lex paused her chopping and cast Hope an evil smile. "Trust me, Hope. By the time we're done with Peggy, she won't dare to speak your name, much less roll around with you on the dirty tile floor for some helium."

"Holy hell." Hope closed her eyes and took in a deep breath. "Please just don't let me end up on the news again. And for goodness sake, don't go all Tonya Harding on her flat butt."

"Tonya Harding?" Lex asked, looking confused.

"You know. The figure skater whose husband went after another skater and took her knee out before a huge competition? They were both Olympians." When Lex didn't respond, Hope said, "Never mind. I'm obviously showing my age. The rules are: Don't physically attack her, don't lie, and don't do anything that will cause me to end up on the news again. Got it?"

"No lies? Really?" Lex asked, sounding exasperated. "After the lies she spread about you?"

"That's just not my lane," Hope said. "Hit her hard with stuff she's actually done. Not fake news."

Lex's eyes glinted as she grinned at Hope. "If dirty laundry is on the table, then don't you worry about one thing. We've got this covered. And man, it's going to be sweet. She was downright hateful to me and Jackson when we were in school. It's going to feel good to bring her down a notch or three."

"I think I've created a monster," Hope mumbled. She

retreated to the living room, finding Grace where she'd left her. "What should I do about Lucas?"

"Isn't it obvious?" Grace asked.

"Uh, clearly it isn't. Otherwise I wouldn't be standing in your living room asking you for advice."

"Go find him. Apologize. Do what you have to in order for him to take you out again tonight, and then get naked again. Only this time, do it in a bed instead of the Pacific Ocean."

Hope started to object, but Grace put her hand up, stopping her.

"If you want to make this right, you have to go apologize. The naked part is optional, depending on how it goes."

She was right. Not about the naked part, but about the apology. She did need to go talk to him. And the sooner the better.

"I think I know where he is," Hope said, more to herself than to her friend.

"Good. Go get him." Grace stood. "Now, I need to help my niece make that meal so I won't be lying when I tell Owen I made it."

Hope chuckled and then left to go find her man.

CHAPTER EIGHTEEN

*I*t didn't take long for Hope to find Lucas. He was right where he always went when he was troubled. The breeze ruffled her hair as she walked up the wooden stairs that led to the Premonition Pointe lighthouse that was located on the south side of town.

He was leaning against the railing, staring out at the churning sea. "I wondered if you'd come find me here."

"Where else would I go?" Hope asked.

He shrugged. "On your date with the surfer?"

"After last night? It was never going to happen." Hope spotted the head of a seal popping up out of the water, and she silently pointed it out to him.

He nodded, indicating that he saw the seal. Then he glanced at her. "He didn't seem to know the date was off."

"That's my fault." She gave him a small smile. "I not only forgot to cancel, I completely forgot I'd even agreed to the date. I'm sure that makes me a horrible person, but you see, the guy I had dinner with last night has been occupying my thoughts."

Lucas let out a grunt and thought, *What I wouldn't give to hear what's going on in that head of yours.*

Hope placed her hand over his and squeezed. "Are you sure about that?"

He didn't even look at her as he answered, "Yes."

Gods, she loved that it didn't bother him that she could sometimes hear his thoughts. A sense of peace washed over her. How did she get so lucky to have people in her life that just accepted her new invasive ability? People who loved her so unconditionally that this change in her life hadn't fazed them in the least. "First off, I've been regretting my decision to go skinny-dipping instead of just taking you back to my place last night."

He turned his hand over and tightened his fingers over hers. "Is that because the entire town is talking about our antics?"

Hope chuckled. "No. I don't really care if they know I've been splashing around naked with you. But it would've made my life easier, and I'd probably be a lot more relaxed." She winked at him.

"There's no probably about it," he said with a chuckle. "What else is going on in that head of yours? I can practically feel the tension rolling off of you."

She sighed heavily. "It appears there's a nasty rumor going around that I trade sexual favors for business opportunities. I had three clients cancel on me today. So imagine my chagrin at the fact that I'm doing the time without ever having done the crime."

"There's a rumor that you're *what*?" Lucas's expression went from shocked to downright pissed. "Who started this rumor?"

"I'm pretty sure it was Peggy Pitsman. She's bitter that

most of the town comes to me to organize their events. The accidental press conference today didn't help any."

"Damn, Hope. I'm so sorry." He turned and wrapped his arms around her, pulling her in close. "I wouldn't have suggested skinny-dipping last night if I'd known this would happen."

"It's not your fault. Honestly, I don't think anyone would've cared if it hadn't been for that damned rumor." She leaned her head against his shoulder.

"What can I do?" he asked, brushing his lips over her cheek.

"Take me out tonight? It turns out that my calendar is suddenly free."

His hold on her tightened and he tucked her head under his chin. "I'd be thrilled. What time should I pick you up?"

"Six."

"You got it." He dipped his head, and when his lips met hers, Hope's entire body melted right into him. The rest of her life might have been falling apart around her, but this thing with Lucas? For whatever reason, it just felt right. Like maybe they were going to finally figure out how to make it work.

LUCAS HELD Hope's hand as they walked Main Street of Premonition Pointe. They'd already had dinner at an intimate Italian place, and they'd decided to head to Bird's Eye Bakery for dessert. Hope was craving their blackberry pie, and Lucas had been all too willing to grab a piece of key lime pie.

"How does it feel to be back in your hometown after living in the city for so long?" Hope asked him.

"Honestly, it's a relief." His eyes crinkled with amusement. "Isn't it funny how what you think you need often turns out to be completely irrelevant?"

Hope frowned at him. "I'm not sure I understand what you're getting at."

"Just that I imagined my life would be complete once I finally proved that I could make it as a furniture designer. Or when I was first featured in a design magazine. Or even when I started receiving invitations to exclusive parties with celebrity chefs and D-list actors."

"Are you trying to make me feel bad about myself or something?" Hope asked with a laugh. "Because literally none of that has happened for me."

"You made it as a gallery owner and then again as an event planner," he countered.

"Well, those aren't exactly the same. Anyone could do that if they put their mind to it."

"But you managed to do both very well. We both know how hard it is to grow and maintain a successful business. You are exceptional at what you do, Hope, and since I'm a client, I'd know."

She rolled her eyes. "I still think you're biased. Anyway, go on with what you were saying. You've made it and are an important furniture designer. You're in high demand by important people, and yet you still don't feel like your life is complete. Why is that? What's missing?"

"Someone to share it with." He cast her a glance and gave her his sexy half smile that always made her bones melt.

"That's pretty cliché, don't you think?" she asked, trying

to keep from losing her mind. This conversation had taken a turn she hadn't expected. Though maybe she should have. It wasn't like he'd been shy about his intentions since he'd arrived back in town.

"It's the truth." He stopped in front of the bakery and turned to face her. "I'm not saying it was the wrong decision for me to leave town or that it was wrong for you to stay here. We all make choices that shape who we become. I don't know what life I'd be living if I'd stayed here. Maybe I'd have become resentful or ended up in a job I hated. Or maybe I'd have married you, and we would've had four kids and just be sending the last one off to college."

"Kids?" Hope shook her head, and her stomach felt as if she'd swallowed a boulder. "I meant it when I told you I wasn't interested in kids. That hasn't changed. Is that what you're going on about? Do you regret not starting a family?"

"No. Not at all. I'm just saying that our life experiences shape us, so I don't want to live in regret. But what I've come to realize is that all of this success I've built for myself feels awfully empty when you're not there to share it with me. I've missed the hell out of you, Hope. And if it isn't clear, I fully intend to repair this relationship and then never let it go again."

Her breath left her as she stared at him dumbfounded. He'd just laid it all out on the line. The ball was in her court, and she didn't know what to do with it. Deep in her heart, she knew she wanted the same thing. "I don't know what to say to that."

"You don't have to say anything, Hope. Just be prepared. Because I'm not giving up."

A slow smile spread across her face as she said, "Okay."

"Okay? What does that mean?"

"It's means I'll be prepared." She lifted up on her tiptoes and kissed him softly on the lips. "Now let's go inside. You promised me pie."

He chuckled. "That I did." He opened the door for her and added, "After you."

CHAPTER NINETEEN

*B*y the time Monday rolled around, two more of Hope's clients had canceled. The local news had run that clip of her admitting to skinny-dipping with Lucas, one of her clients, no less than half a dozen times. Then they'd followed up the story by informing their viewers that Hope had been spotted with Lucas that same night and then again having brunch together on Sunday morning, adding plenty of fuel to the fire.

Still, she didn't regret a thing. Her evening with Lucas had been perfect. After dessert, he took her home and they sat on her porch, listening to the waves crashing in the distance. He told her stories of his time in Boston, and she talked about closing the art gallery and starting up the event planning business so that she could have more freedom, both with her time and finances. Operating a brick and mortar store had started to wear on her. He'd chuckled and said he understood completely.

She'd considered inviting him in, but after his declaration, she decided it was better to take things slow. She wanted to be one hundred percent sure she was just as ready as he was to commit to their relationship before she started down that path. Sex with him would only cloud her judgment.

Besides, she'd told him, she didn't want his truck parked out in front of her house all night after the spectacle in the square that day. The last thing she needed was to add credence to the rumors that she was sleeping with her clients. And thank the gods that he hadn't slept over. She could only imagine what the news would've reported had someone spotted his truck the next morning.

Small towns, she thought with disgust. Normally she loved knowing everyone. Having that connection. But some days, she wanted nothing more than for Lucas to whisk her away off to Boston where no one knew her. But she'd never been able to leave home before. What made her think she could do it now? She put the thought out of her mind and headed to her appointment with Skyler. The bright spot of her morning was that he hadn't canceled. She'd even called to confirm, just to make sure. They had a dog wedding to plan.

"Hey, hey! Hope. Over here." Skyler jumped up out of his chair and waved with both hands to get Hope's attention.

She grinned instantly and chuckled. It wasn't as if Pointe of View Café was so busy that she wouldn't have easily found him, but she did enjoy his enthusiasm. The gorgeous designer was wearing plaid pants, a coral shirt, and matching suspenders. "You look amazing," she said as she leaned in and gave him a quick hug.

"So do you." He scanned her body, eyeing her critically.

"Except I was expecting something a little more risqué considering your reputation." He gave her an exaggerated wink and then threw his head back and laughed.

"Real cute, Skyler," she said, rolling her eyes. "Better be careful or pretty soon you'll be caught up in my rumor mill. Are you sure you want to chance it?"

"Hell, yes. It's not everyday someone mistakes me for a straight man. That would be a hoot."

It was her turn to look at him critically. "I'm pretty sure that never happens."

He grinned. "I like you."

"I like you, too."

"Now let me get you something to drink," he said, already moving toward the counter. "What do you like?"

"You don't have to do that. I'm usually the one who takes care of—"

"Don't argue with me, Hope. I'm getting a double vanilla extra whip latte. What are you having?" he insisted, giving her a death glare.

"Caramel mocha."

"Extra whip?" he asked with one raised eyebrow.

She laughed. "Yes."

"Thought so." He spun around and headed to the counter. When he returned, he handed her the largest coffee mug she'd ever seen and a piece of coffee cake. "I thought you could use a little indulgence today. I know I would if I were you."

"Are the rumors that bad?" she asked and took a sip of the sweet concoction. "Holy crap, this is going to send me to an early grave, isn't it?"

"At least you'll die happy."

Hope nodded. "Very true. This is delicious. Thank you."

"You're welcome." He took a sip from his own gigantic mug and then leaned forward on his forearms. "What did you do to the wretched Peggy Pitsman?"

Hope held up her hands and shook her head. "Other than be a better event organizer than her, I have no idea."

"She is one green-eyed monster. You would not believe the stories she was telling about you yesterday. I wanted to scratch her eyes out." The look on his face was murderous, and Hope almost laughed. She'd only met the man once, and he was already being just as protective as Grace and Lex.

"More sexual favors crap?" Hope asked with a groan.

"Nope. Well, actually yes, she started in on that, but Pete told a story about how he slept his way to the top and didn't regret it for a second. Then he suggested that she give it a try before she made any judgment calls." Skyler snorted. "You should've seen the look on her face. She looked like she'd just gulped down sour milk."

Hope could barely hold back a giggle when she asked, "Did he really say that?"

"Which part?" Skyler's eyes gleamed with amusement.

"The part about sleeping his way to the top and suggesting she try it?"

"Hell, yes. Pete can't stand snotty bitches like her."

"Is it true?" she asked, giving him a skeptical look.

Skyler snickered. "Yes and no. Pete did shag his boss before we met, but that's not why he was promoted. He's brilliant at what he does. He just wanted to shut her up. Too bad it didn't work."

"Oh, what else did she say?" Hope felt herself tense. If Peggy Pitsman wasn't going to let up on her attack, Hope would have no choice other than to go to war. It wasn't a place she wanted to be, but she could not sit back and let Peggy destroy her reputation.

"She tried to tell us that your last three events ended with most of the attendees getting food poisoning."

"What?" Hope nearly came out of her chair. "You can't be serious? Nothing could be further from the truth."

"I know," he said with conviction. "You don't think I'd let just anyone plan our dog wedding, do you? I know how to check to make sure I'm working with the best."

Hope couldn't help it. Tears stung the backs of her eyes. It felt too damned good to have someone see through the bullshit and stick with her despite the ugly rumors. "Thank you."

"No need to thank me," he said, reaching across the table and briefly squeezing her fingers. "Because, honey, I'm probably going to be your most high-maintenance client ever. Don't be surprised if I call you at all hours of the day. I just can't help it when my brain gets going."

Hope groaned. "You really are gonna be a pain in my ass, aren't you?"

"Yep. But you're gonna love me anyway because I'm loyal and fun, and I'll cut a bitch if they deserve it." He gave her a cheeky smile, making her laugh.

"I think I can accept those terms. Now, let's get to work. I brought notes." She pulled a file out of her bag and put it on the table.

"That's good," Skyler said, his green eyes flashing with mischief as he reached for something in a messenger bag she hadn't noticed and produced a file twice as large as hers. "Cause so did I."

Hope dropped her head down to the table and laughed.

When she popped back up, she cocked her head to the side and said, "You're adorable, you know that?"

"I'm glad you think so, because this is right about the time when most people start running." His tone was light, but there was a hint of seriousness in the delivery, and she had no trouble believing that he was just a little too extra for some people.

"No way. We're besties now whether you like it or not. You and Pete took on my nemesis. There's no better bonding ritual than that."

"Did I say I like you?" he asked.

"Yes, you did. No getting out of it now."

"What I meant to say is that I love you." He held his pinky finger out to her. "We need to pinky swear our loyalty."

Feeling lighter and better than she had in forty-eight hours, she wrapped her pinky finger around his and said, "Pinky swear."

He repeated her words and then opened his file. "Time to get to work. What do you think of these felted replicas? I was thinking they could be used in the center pieces."

Hope glanced at the picture of a mini felted dog that looked exactly like the real live dog sitting next to it. She frowned. "Really? They look like voodoo dogs."

Skyler glanced at the picture again and then grimaced. "You know what? You're right." He crumpled up the paper and tossed it over his shoulder. "I knew hiring you was a good call."

"I'll have to remember to thank Gigi for the invite, because I love that you brought all this." Hope waved to his folder. "We're gonna have so much fun."

"Girl," he said, his voice going up an octave. "You have no idea."

CHAPTER TWENTY

"It seems like we should have the blood of our ancestors for this ritual," Joy said, eyeing the red wine as she swirled it in her glass. She was sitting cross-legged on the cliff, the fire they'd conjured flickering in her blue eyes.

Hope had been studying her, trying to decide how she was doing. Joy had been scarce the last few days, and Hope had started to suspect that the reality of Paul leaving had finally come crashing down on her. But after that statement she had to force herself to not burst out laughing. "Uh, Joy, I know we're witches, but do we really want to put in that much effort? Remember the last time we conjured blood from the dusty old bones of our relatives?"

"From dusty old bones?" Gigi asked, looking a little green around the edges.

"You know," Grace said conversationally, "it probably would help bind us together better."

"I think wine is probably good enough," Gigi said nervously as she wiped a hand on her cotton skirt. "I mean, we wouldn't want to disturb the spirits if we don't have to, right?"

Joy let out a cackle and then quickly clasped her hand over her mouth. "Sorry. It's just too funny."

Hope and Grace gave in to the humor and started laughing with her.

"Oh, very funny," Gigi said dryly. "It's always fun to pick on the new girl, right?"

"Yes," the three of them said in unison.

"You might as well get used to it," Grace said mildly. "You're joining our coven. The three of us are never going to let up."

"But the good news is that you'll always have three sisters to count on for anything," Joy added, squeezing her hand.

Hope nodded thoughtfully, adding, "And we'll be ready to avenge you, should some jackhole decide to try to ruin your reputation because she's a jealous bitch who can't seem to find success on her own even though she's had every privilege bestowed on her, including a husband who bankrolls her operation."

"Oh, boy. That was specific," Grace muttered.

Hope let out a bark of humorless laughter. "Sorry. Excuse my rant. If you couldn't tell, Peggy Pitsman has gotten on my very last nerve." Hope had almost lost another client and had spent the better part of her day convincing her that no, she wasn't using substandard caterers who'd been closed down by the health department three times.

"We could curse Peggy," Grace suggested. "I'm particularly good at STD curses if you remember correctly."

Hope and Joy burst out laughing, but Gigi seemed to shrink away from her.

"Don't worry," Hope said. "Grace didn't do it on purpose.

It was a case of wishing a curse into existence without her even casting a spell. Strong emotions can make that happen every now and then, and Grace's husband had just left her for the office assistant. Is it any wonder she wished they'd both get genital warts?"

"Oh, my goodness." Gigi started giggling and then laughed so hard she fell backward onto the earth and held her stomach until she finally got a hold of herself. "Grace. That's too much. Dammit, now I'm disappointed you didn't wish them on my ex."

"So am I to be honest," Grace said, holding her wine glass up in a mock toast. "Next time?"

"Next time," Gigi agreed.

Grace glanced at Joy. "What about you? Any special requests for Paul? Herpes? Warts? Boils?"

"Boils? Oh. Em. Gee. He'd die." Joy snickered at the thought but then shook her head. "As lovely as that sounds, I think it's best to leave that alone. I don't need any fuel added to the fire until after the divorce."

"Good call," Gigi said, holding up her glass the way Grace had a few moments ago. "Keep it civil until the papers are signed. Then all bets are off."

Since Gigi was recently divorced, it was no surprise she related the most to what Joy was going through. Though Gigi had thrown her husband out. Joy hadn't asked for hers to leave.

"Fine. No boils." Grace stood and swept her auburn hair behind her in a loose ponytail. "But we can wish for him to regrow his brain, right? Because anyone stupid enough to leave Joy obviously fried something in his head. Maybe it was all the number crunching."

"Or porn," Hope mumbled.

"I heard that," Joy said, but there wasn't any heat behind her words. "Honestly, I don't care why he left anymore. If he doesn't want me, then he can go. I deserve so much better."

"Hear, hear!" The other three witches chanted and raised their glasses in unison.

Joy held hers up as well. "Looks like we're ready to officially add our fourth sister. Hope? You ready?"

"Yep." Hope scanned the four wine glasses they were all holding up and said, "Levitate."

All four of the glasses slipped from their hands and floated high in front of them, right over the glowing flames of the small fire they'd built.

Hope held out her hands to her coven mates. "Time to form the physical circle."

They followed suit until all four of them were connected as one unit.

"One of four, four of one, tonight we celebrate the sister we've won." Hope grinned at Gigi. "She walked into our lives during a tumultuous time in her personal life, but even in those early days when her future seemed unclear, all three of us knew her future belonged right here… with us."

"That's right," Grace said.

"Wouldn't want it any other way," Joy added.

"So tonight, we raise our glasses to the sky, ask that the wine within be blessed by our higher power, and then drink to lifelong sisterhood where we will always stand for one another, hold one another, and lift one another up with everything we have."

The wine in the glasses turned a bright, blood red and then quickly turned back to its original red wine color. One glass floated to each of the witches, and without the help of their hands, the glasses tilted, making their offerings to the union. They each opened their mouths, took the dram of wine, and swallowed.

The fire suddenly shot up higher and turned a brilliant white. The wood crackled, sending off four sparks that quickly turned into four interconnected rings that hung right in the middle of the four witches.

They stood staring at the rings until finally, Hope snapped her fingers and the white fire rings floated back down to the fire and disappeared in the flames.

All three of them studied Gigi, who just stood there looking stunned.

"Well, do you feel different?" Grace asked.

Gigi blinked at them. "Did you really just say I'm going to be stuck with you three for eternity?" Her expression turned to one of pure horror.

"Um, yeah. That's what happens when you join a coven. I thought—" Hope started, but she was cut off by Gigi's laughter.

"I'm just kidding. You did say you're going to needle me for the foreseeable future, didn't you? I just wanted to test it out."

Grace and Joy laughed.

"One thing's for sure," Hope said, chuckling. "You fit right in."

"And thank the gods for that," Gigi said, holding her arms out wide. "Now give your newest sister a hug."

They all moved in, wrapping their arms around each other. It felt good. Peaceful. And just right. It always did when she was with her coven.

Just as Hope was pulling away, her phone buzzed.

"Really, Hope?" Grace admonished. "What if that thing had gone off during the ritual?"

"Sorry!" Hope exclaimed, feeling like an idiot. They had a strict policy. No phones allowed during coven meetings. She went to just turn it off, but then she caught Lex's name on the screen. The ringing stopped and a text came through immediately. *Call me. It's urgent.*

Hope didn't hesitate. She hit Lex's number. "What happened?"

"It's Peggy Pitsman's daughter. She overdosed tonight."

CHAPTER TWENTY-ONE

"*L*ex?" Grace called as she strode out the back door of her cottage with Hope on her heels. Joy and Gigi were in the house making coffee and giving them time to talk to Lex before they all converged on her. When Lex had called, she'd been really shaken up over the night's events.

"Over here," Jackson said from where he sat with Lex on the outdoor loveseat. She had her knees drawn up and her arms wrapped around them.

Grace hurried over to her niece and kneeled in front of her. "Are you all right?"

Lex nodded, but Jackson, who had his arm wrapped around her shoulders and her head tucked against his chest, shook his head.

"What happened?"

Hope grabbed a couple of the deck chairs and pulled them over so she and Grace could sit near Lex. Once they were both seated, Hope reached over and took one of Lex's hands. They didn't have any details other than she and

Jackson had been at the Beachside Beer Garden when Peggy's daughter went into a seizure from an apparent overdose.

"I had the night off, so I called Jackson to see if he wanted to get together, and we ended up at the Beachside Beer Garden," Lex said.

"Bronwyn is out of town helping her college roommate plan a wedding," Jackson explained.

Lex glanced up at him. "You know that's not the only reason I called."

"Of course not," he said soothingly. "Besties for life."

She gave him a shaky smile and turned her attention back to Grace. "Anyway, we were sitting out on the patio when Whitley walked in with a couple of her friends. We waved, but that's it. They were sitting a few tables away from us, laughing too loudly and being somewhat obnoxious, the way people do when they've had a few too many."

"Lex and I were actually counting the times Whitley and her friends yelled *party*," Jackson said. "When the count got over a dozen, we lost interest. I went in to settle our tab, and that's when all hell broke loose."

"I've never seen anything like that before," Lex said as she shuddered. She closed her eyes for a moment and then continued. "Right about the time Jackson went inside, Whitley's friends got up and ran down the beach. They were yelling something about finding mermen. Whitley got up to follow them, but she stumbled and started to shake violently as she crashed to the patio."

"That sounds terrifying," Grace said gently.

Lex wiped at her eyes. "I was the nearest person to her, so I ran to her side and tried to make sure she didn't hurt herself on any of the chairs or tables. The paramedics showed up a few minutes later. I heard them say something about an overdose. I'd been thinking epilepsy or something, but they administered some drug to counteract the effects of whatever she took and then carried her away."

"I heard them say she was exhibiting all the signs of an ashe overdose," Jackson said.

"Ashe?" Hope asked, frowning. "What's that?"

"The new drug circulating through town that's causing all the overdoses," Jackson said. "It comes in a compressed block that people burn like incense in a glass pipe, and they inhale the smoke."

"And it's enough to cause an overdose? What the heck is it made out of?" Hope asked, feeling like she was a hundred years old. Compressed blocks? She'd never heard of a drug like that.

"It must be," Lex said, sitting up and wiping at her eyes. "That's not something I ever want to see again."

"I can imagine." Grace leaned over and gave her a hug.

"Does anyone know how Whitley's doing? Or if anyone called her mother?" Hope asked. Peggy Pitsman wasn't her favorite person, but the woman needed to know her daughter had been taken to the hospital.

"Lex tried to call the hospital, but they wouldn't give her any information," Jackson said. "We didn't think to call her mom. I guess I assumed the hospital would do that."

Hope pulled her phone out of her pocket and dialed the woman's number. It rang four times and then went to voicemail. "Peggy, this is Hope Anderson. You've probably already been called, but I just wanted to make sure you were aware that Whitley was taken to the hospital this evening after an apparent overdose. We don't have any information other than that. We all hope she's okay. Take care."

"You're a good person, Hope," Grace said.

"Not that good. But sometimes, you just have to do what you have to do," she said stoically. She was still over-the-top pissed at Peggy's antics, but Whitley deserved to have her mother there when she woke up.

"Truth," Jackson said, standing to let Grace sit next to Lex.

Grace tucked herself beside her niece and pulled her into a reassuring hug.

"Hope, can I talk to you for a second?" Jackson asked.

"Sure." Hope rose and followed Jackson into the house.

Gigi and Joy were sitting at Grace's table with mugs in front of them.

"Hey," Joy said, jumping up and running to the coffee pot. "We peeked out the window and saw that Lex is pretty upset, so we wanted to give her some space."

"She is." Jackson pulled one of the chairs out and sat heavily. "It was pretty brutal. After the seizure, Whitley was so pale, I was afraid for a moment that she…" He swallowed hard. "I was afraid we'd lost her."

"I'm so sorry, Jackson," Gigi said leaning forward to pat his hand. "She must be a good friend of yours."

He shook his head. "No. Not at all. We were in the same class, but she and Lex didn't really get along that well, so we steered clear of each other. I'm just shaken up because that's the third person I've watched overdose on ashe, and it's terrifying. You'd think after four people were hospitalized that most would stay away from it, but it doesn't look like that's been a deterrent."

"Oh, no. That's terrible," Gigi said, covering her mouth and leaning back in her chair. "I'm so sorry you both had to witness that tonight. Is Whitley all right?"

"I don't know," he said as he accepted a cup of coffee from Joy.

She leaned down, wrapped her arm around his shoulders, and gave him a hug. "If you need anything, let me know, okay?"

Jackson had spent many afternoons in Joy's home as a kid. He and his mother had moved in next door to Joy and her family when he was just five years old. He and Kyle, her youngest son, had been friends ever since.

He covered one of her hands with one of his own. "Thanks Mrs. Lansing."

"It's Joy. You know that."

He smiled up at her and nodded. "Thanks, Joy."

Holding her own mug of coffee, Hope sat across from Jackson. "You said you wanted to talk to me? Is this okay, or do you want to go somewhere more private?"

"This is fine." He gave Gigi and Joy a small smile. "I just didn't want to talk about this in front of Lex right now. She's really shaken up."

"Yeah." Hope glanced out the window and spotted Lex and Grace sitting on the love seat and talking quietly. "I'm pretty sure Grace will be able to calm her nerves."

"I hope so." He took a long sip of his coffee and closed his eyes for a moment. "This is really good."

"That's because I spiked it with Irish whiskey," Joy said with a wink.

He glanced at his mug and then chuckled. "That would do it." Jackson took another sip, ran a hand through his dark curly hair, and then turned to Hope. "I tracked Spencer down, the guy who overdosed in Pointe of View Café the other morning."

185

"How is he?" Hope recalled the tall young man and how out of it he was the day he'd collapsed right in from of them.

"He's doing much better, but he's not talking. He wouldn't tell the doctors where he got the drug. Can you believe he claimed he walked into a room where they were smoking something and that's how he inhaled too much?" Jackson rolled his eyes. "Like that's going to be enough to take someone down. And where exactly was this party that was going on before ten in the morning? I think he was afraid of getting into legal trouble. He wouldn't even tell me. Said he didn't want to be the source of anyone else getting their hands on it."

"I can't blame him for that, I guess," Hope said, trying to ignore the frustration causing her shoulders to tense. She understood Spencer's reasons. But ignoring the problem wasn't going to make it go away on its own. "Any leads on the other two who overdosed?"

Jackson nodded, his eyes suddenly looking tired. "Yeah. I got their names from my gossip sources. I was planning on hitting them up tomorrow, if I can find them that is."

"I really appreciate this, Jackson," Hope said, meaning it. His thoughts were whirling, but they weren't exactly coherent. Mostly he was longing for his bed and the opportunity to put everything out of his mind. "Why don't you go on home and get some rest," she told him. "We've got it from here."

"You have no idea how much I want to do just that," he said, frowning. "But there's something else I need to tell you."

"Okay." She glanced at both Gigi and Joy. They were giving him their undivided attention, both of them with worried expressions on their faces.

"That thing Lex and I were going to do, to out Peggy Pitsman?" he said with a grimace.

"Yeah?" She'd completely forgotten that they'd promised they had something on her. Now that her daughter was in the hospital, going after Peggy was out of the question, no matter what she'd done to Hope. "Whatever it is, please can you just keep it to yourself for now?"

"That's what I'm trying to tell you. It's too late. I already gave the story to the *Premonition Perspective*. It's supposed to run tomorrow." His expression turned pained. "I called the reporter and tried to stop it, but she said it already went to print. It's too late."

"Oh, damn." Hope closed her eyes and sat back in her chair. "How bad is it?"

"It's bad," he breathed and let his head drop back. "I feel really shitty right now."

"You couldn't have known," Gigi said, trying to soothe him. But Hope was certain nothing was going to help at that point. She could almost feel the guilt seeping off of him.

"What is the article going to say?" she asked, realizing that they just needed to rip the bandage off.

"Peggy Pitsman had an affair with the girls' basketball coach when we were in high school. The story is about how she slept with him in order to convince him to start Whitley instead of Lex."

Hope was speechless for a few seconds, her mouth working as if she were going to say something but no words came out.

"You can't be serious," Joy said, her eyes wide. "Peggy Pitsman slept with Mr. Gale? The same Mr. Gale who was married to Brenda, the one who brought homemade cupcakes to all the booster meetings and was just about the sweetest person who ever lived?"

He nodded, looking miserable. "I'm just glad she won't have to see the story tomorrow. She didn't deserve how he treated her."

Brenda had passed away a couple of years ago after suffering a massive heart attack.

"This isn't just a rumor is it? Do you have proof?" Hope finally asked.

"I have proof. I promised you I would." He pulled out his phone, tapped a few buttons, and then showed her a picture that was clearly Peggy and Mr. Gale wrapped up in a compromising position in his office. There was a whiteboard behind him that had *West Coast Tournament Champs* and the year scrawled across it. "I took this photo myself when we were still in school. Afterward, Lex and I spied on them a lot. We both heard her offer him a roll in the sack as long as Whitley started in the next game. And sure enough, despite having a horrible season, Whitley started instead of Lex."

Joy let out a gasp and covered her mouth. Then she narrowed her eyes in pure anger. "I remember that. Lex was so upset. And then when the team was down twenty points, he put her in, and she nearly killed herself to get them back in the lead. That happened a number of times that season. We never understood why. Mr. Gale is getting a piece of my mind tomorrow, that's for sure."

Hope stared at her friend and almost laughed. It wasn't as if Lex was her daughter. Though they all loved her. Lex was family, and it was no surprise Joy was protective. Hope just couldn't believe she'd remembered all of that. "I didn't know you were such a basketball fan, Joy. Did you go to all the games?"

"Yes. I met Grace there and we watched Lex's game and then Kyle's which was right afterward. I've been a huge fan ever since, though I prefer the college games to the pros. It's just more interesting."

"Huh. How come I never knew that?" Hope asked.

"Basketball wasn't your thing. You were busy building your business." Joy smiled at her.

"I guess so." Hope cleared her throat and turned to Jackson. "Thanks for letting me know. I don't love that this is coming out tomorrow. But it can't be helped, so try not to stress about it, okay?"

"I'll try." He sucked in a deep breath. "I just feel so petty right now."

"Don't. She started this by spreading untrue rumors about me." Hope shook her head in disgust. "And isn't it just so predictable that she projected her immorality on me."

"That's always the way it goes down, isn't it?" Gigi said. "They're never original."

The was a murmur of agreement, and then Jackson slipped out the back door to say goodnight to Lex.

The three witches stared at each other.

"Now what?" Joy asked. "Should we be doing more interviews around town? Or do we just sit back and wait for Jackson to talk to the two other people who overdosed?"

"I think we wait. Tomorrow's going to be ugly when that article comes out. I think it's better to lay low," Hope said.

"Got it." Joy turned her attention to her coffee mug.

Gigi sat back in her chair and said, "Well, that was one hell of an initiation into the coven. But when do we get to start hexing people?"

Hope and Joy stared at her.

She started to laugh. "I'm just kidding. I only hex people

189

on Sundays." She gave them a cheeky grin and stood. "I'm headed home. Call me if you need me to cast a flatulence spell on some jackhole. It's my specialty." Then she waved and strode out of the house as if she hadn't just dropped the bomb that she was skilled at giving people gas.

Hope started to chuckle and then dropped her head to the table when her chuckle turned into a giggle fit. Joy joined her until they both had tears in their eyes. Hope sat up straight, wiped her eyes, and said, "I'm really going to enjoy her."

CHAPTER TWENTY-TWO

"Oh. Em. Gee. Polly will loooove these," Skyler exclaimed while staring into the case at Four Paws Barkery. The shop had everything from freshly baked treats to one-of-a-kind dog and cat outfits that had been made by the owner.

"Cake pops? Those would work great since they have sticks that we can arrange in a floral foam, but we'll need to be diligent that no pups get too excited and try to chomp that down too. It will cause waste we don't need."

"Hope," he said, looking at her like she'd lost her mind. "The sticks are edible too. See?" He pointed inside the case to the sign that was hard to miss.

"Ahhh. Oops. I guess I'm just a little distracted. Sorry." Hope had almost forgotten that they'd made a date to check out the barkery, as well as the party supply store. She'd been so worried about the story that was coming out in the *Perspective* that she hadn't even checked her appointment book that morning. In fact, if he hadn't called to tell her he was running late, she might not have remembered at all.

"What's with you today?" he asked, studying her. "Your energy is really off. Like, so off that I'm thinking we need to get massages after this to snap you out of it."

Hope let out a little moan at the thought of someone working the tension out of her upper back and shoulders. "There really isn't anything I'd like better."

"Good. We'll go after we're done here. Lance will find a way to fit us in." He rubbed his hands together as if he were warming up to perform some delicate surgery. Then he just pulled his phone out and called their favorite spa owner.

The bell chimed on the door, and heavy footsteps sounded behind them. The scent of antiseptic permeated the air, making Hope wrinkle her nose as she turned to see who was barreling through the store like a bull in a china shop.

Peggy Pitsman. And she was headed straight for Hope.

"Hope Anderson! I know you're responsible for this. How dare you do this to me, especially after what happened last night. You truly are the devil, aren't you?" She waved the *Premonition Perspective* in Hope's face while pointing a shaky finger at her.

"Whoa, back the eff up, lady. No one talks to my friend like that," Skyler said, stepping between the two of them and forcing Peggy to retreat.

"But she's spreading vicious rumors about me," Peggy cried.

Skyler raised one skeptical eyebrow. "The way I heard it is that you were the one making up lies about Hope. Projection much?"

Peggy pressed her lips together, and her face turned bright red.

Hope was certain that if she kept it up, her head would explode.

"I am not projecting," Peggy said through clenched teeth. She craned her neck to see around Skyler. "I expect you to have a full retraction printed in the next issue with an apology. Better yet, you march down to the local radio show right now and tell everyone this is a complete fabrication."

"Hold on right there—" Skyler started.

"I've got this," Hope said, cutting him off and then giving him a ghost of a smile. Hope loved and appreciated that her new friend was defending her with complete conviction, despite not knowing if she was behind the article or not. Clearly, they were going to be great friends. "Peggy, I didn't have anything to do with that article being written or printed. If I asked for a retraction, they'd show me the door. And as far as the radio program, what makes you think anyone in this town would believe me anyway? Last I heard, I was hiring caterers who serve spoiled food and using sex to book my clients. I'd think you'd want someone a little more respectable to champion your virtue."

"Damn. She told you," Skyler sing-songed and snapped his fingers at Peggy, almost making Hope laugh. But then she sobered when she remembered that Whitley was likely still in the hospital.

Peggy crinkled the paper in her fist and then threw it on the ground. "I know you're behind this. Mark my words; I'll find out how, and then everyone will know what an uncaring bitch you are." One tear spilled down her cheek, and she angrily brushed it away.

"I was sorry to hear about your daughter. How is she today?" Hope asked gently.

"None of your business," Peggy spat. "I can't believe you're asking me that after your friend's niece gave her those drugs." Then she thought, *if only that were the case, then I could make sure this never happens again.*

Hope studied her, letting her own anger go. This was a mother in pain, and she was lashing out at her only real target. That was fine. Hope could take it. "We both know Lex didn't give your daughter drugs. She was the only one who was there to help her when she went down because Whitley's so-called friends had run out on her. Why don't we call a truce and try to figure out who might have supplied her with drugs?"

"My daughter doesn't hang out with druggies," Peggy insisted, refusing to listen to reason.

"Right," Skyler said from behind them.

Hope agreed with him but didn't push it. "Peggy, how is Whitley? Is she going to be okay?"

Peggy shot daggers at her with just her gaze. But finally, she let out a sigh of disgust and said, "Yes. She should come home tomorrow."

"I'm really glad to hear that," Hope said. "I mean that. I hope she recovers quickly."

Peggy nodded and turned on her heel to leave. But right before she reached the door, she turned again and stared Hope in the eye. "I need to find out who's behind these drugs. Will you help me?"

Hope wanted to deck the woman. Just a few moments ago, she'd asked Peggy for information on where her daughter might have gotten drugs, but she'd completely ignored the question. Nothing good would come from the two of them working together. "I don't think so. I don't even know why you think I'd know anyway. I don't do drugs. Why would I have any information?"

"Please, Hope," she said, and tears shone in her eyes. She

sniffed and continued, "Everyone knows you asked Gabrielle, that reporter from the *Premonition Pointe News*, to look into the overdoses in this town. I don't know who else to ask for help. The police made a report, but they said unless someone comes forward there isn't much they can do. I just want to protect my daughter. Please, I don't have anyone else to turn to."

Damn, how can Hope say no to that? Skyler thought.

She couldn't, but it had more to do with the desperation in her tone than the actual words. And since Hope already had people helping her try to find the source of the drugs, she nodded.

"Really?" Peggy said, her eyes wide in surprise.

"Yes, but I have conditions," Hope said, crossing her arms over her chest and staring Peggy down.

Peggy gulped. "What conditions?"

"First," Hope held up one finger, "you will take out an entire page ad in the newspaper to apologize for spreading the rumor that guests got food poisoning after attending my events."

"I didn't start that rumor," Peggy insisted. The way she glanced away and turned red again would have been enough to convince Hope that she was lying, but when Peggy thought about the day she'd told Yasmeen an elaborate story about five people running to the bathroom at the same time, she unknowingly confirmed it.

"Yes you did. I bet Yasmeen would back me up if pressed," Hope said.

Peggy grimaced. "Okay, fine. It did start with me. But it was a joke. Yasmeen wasn't supposed to take it seriously. I was just frustrated because one wedding shower canceled after the bride got cold feet and the baby shower I'd just done was a complete bust after only one guest showed up. I was having a bad day, okay? I didn't think Yasmeen would take me seriously. I really am sorry." Her shoulders slumped as she added, "I'll get them to run a statement tomorrow."

"That settles number one then," Hope said with a nod and held up two fingers. "Secondly, you need to stop telling people I sleep with my clients. It's a blatant lie, and if you persist, I'll file a defamation lawsuit."

Peggy's posture straightened, and there was conviction in her tone when she said, "I absolutely didn't start that rumor."

Hope studied her and opened her mind, trying to get a glimpse of what the woman was thinking. Hope bristled when Peggy's thoughts came through loud and clear. *Starting a rumor isn't the same thing as repeating it, right?* Hope rolled her eyes. This woman was something else.

"You slept with your clients?" Skyler asked in an awed voice. "Now I know we're going to be besties. I love a dirty girl."

"Skyler," she said, unable to control the amusement that rolled through her. "Sorry to disappoint you, but I don't sleep with my clients. If you don't want to be my bestie anymore, I understand."

He let out an exaggerated huff. "Well, that's disappointing, but I guess we can still give it a go."

She chuckled.

"What about Lucas King?" Peggy asked, eyeing her.

Now Peggy was just crossing the line. "Lucas and I have a long history, as you well know. But I'll be damned if I let you pry into my private life. What Lucas and I do is no one's concern but our own."

"Except when you go skinny-dipping right out in the

open where everyone can see you," Peggy said, clearly unable to help herself.

"Maybe try minding your own business for once," Hope said. "Are we done here? I'll do whatever I can to find out who is supplying our young people with ashe, and you'll print a retraction about the food poisoning in the paper and stop spreading rumors about me, regardless of where they originate. Deal?" Hope held her hand out to the other woman.

Peggy hesitated, staring at Hope's hand. Then she slowly reached out and shook it. "Deal."

Hope and Skyler watched her go until the door closed behind her.

"She's a pill," he said.

"Tell me about it." Hope sank down onto an ottoman that had the words *Puppy's Domain* stitched on the side.

Skyler sat next to her, stretching out his legs and crossing them at the ankles. He was so handsome and stylish that he was almost painful to look at. Meanwhile, Hope was wearing leggings and an oversized sweatshirt that made her look like she'd given up on anything other than comfort.

"I love your shoes," she said, eyeing his saddle shoes.

"Me too," he said excitedly. "They're new."

She grinned at him, and silence fell between them again until Skyler asked, "Have you really never slept with a client?"

"Never," she confirmed.

"Besides Lucas King, right?"

She cast him a sidelong glance. "Not since he's been back in town. No, I haven't."

"Why not? That man is *hot*," he said.

"It's complicated," she said with a sigh.

"Doesn't look complicated from where I sit," he said, patting her hand. "Looks to me like you two are always going to be drawn together. From what I've pieced together from listening to the town gossip—"

"You can't trust those lies," she insisted.

"True, but I'm good at reading between the lines. Let's see if I've got it straight."

She pursed her lips and raised one eyebrow, indicating she was skeptical. "You can try. But if I laugh, don't take it personally. These types of guesses always make me chuckle."

"Excellent." He turned to face her head-on. "It looks to me like he's your childhood sweetheart. Right?"

She nodded.

"Then he was likely your first everything. Or at the very least, the first person you were in love with."

"Yeah."

"Then he left for college and you broke up. Fast forward a few years. He shows back up in town, and you two pick up where you left off until he left town for a job."

"What are you getting at, Skyler?" she asked, not enjoying the trip down memory lane.

"You two are magnetic together. Fighting it is useless. And if you've found the one who sees all your facets and loves you because of them, then that's the one to hold on to. Hold on and never let go, Hope. Love is the only thing that really matters in this life. Hold on with both hands and never let go."

There were tears in her eyes as she listened to him. She was choked up and suddenly really needed to see Lucas. "I need to go."

He leaned in and gave her a kiss on the cheek. "I know you do. Get going. I'll cancel your massage appointment."

Damn, she'd really been looking forward to that. But when she thought of Lucas and telling him how she felt, her heart fluttered in her chest and the tension disappeared from her body for the first time since Lucas had rolled back into town.

CHAPTER TWENTY-THREE

ope pulled her Toyota Highlander to a stop in front of the two-story craftsman that she'd always imagined herself living in one day. When Lucas had purchased it, she'd felt that it was a sucker punch in the gut. He knew how much she loved the place. They'd talked about it often enough when they were younger. But now she knew he'd bought it with the intention of winning her back.

A few weeks ago, she'd have recoiled at that thought. Maybe even thought it was manipulative. But now? The gesture felt sincere. Like he finally was ready to commit to a life with her in Premonition Pointe and was willing to prove it in any way he could.

"Hope Anderson?" Bell King called from the flower garden as Hope started to make her way up the path. A couple of dogs started barking from around the side of the house, and Hope assumed Lucas's two labs were in his yard.

Hope smiled at Lucas's mom. They'd been close back when she and Lucas dated and had remained friendly over the years. "Hey, Ms. K."

"It's about time you came to see me." She held her arms out, inviting a hug.

Hope embraced her, and they held each other for a long moment. "How are you doing?" Hope asked her.

"Really good. I'll be even better when Lucas finally comes to visit me."

"What do you mean?" Hope asked as she pulled back to study her.

"Oh, you know. Since he moved to Boston, I don't see him that much. I miss my boy." Bell took Hope by the arm and led her up the path to the front door. "Come in. I'll make us some tea and we'll sit on the porch and catch up."

Hope wasn't sure what to say or do. Lucas had told her that his mom had early stage dementia. Her illness was the catalyst that brought him back to town. But this was the first time she'd witnessed it.

"Hope? Are you ready to go in?" Bell asked.

She nodded and followed the woman she'd once considered her second mother into the house.

"Bell?" a woman called from the back of the house.

"That's Janie," Bell whispered to Hope. "She's the woman Lucas hired to keep an eye on me when he's not here."

Hope nodded, trying to fit the pieces together. Just a few seconds ago, it seemed Bell thought Lucas still lived in Boston, yet she knew that Janie was her caretaker. "Where *is* Lucas?" she tried.

"He's meeting a client about some custom cabinets," Bell said with a proud smile as she took a seat in an armchair.

"It's custom built-ins," the woman Hope assumed was Janie said as she emerged into the living room, carrying two glasses of lemonade. She was tall with long dark locks and was dressed in a cotton skirt and tank top. Janie looked more like someone Hope would find selling handmade soap at the farmer's market than an in-home caregiver.

Bell took her glass and frowned. "I could have sworn he told me cabinets." Then she chuckled. "It's so hard to keep his schedule straight these days."

Janie handed Hope the second glass and nodded at Bell. "He is a busy guy, but he's usually home in time for dinner. Can't complain about that."

"You're right." Bell nodded and glanced at her lemonade. "Oops, I promised Hope tea."

"It's okay. This is perfect," Hope said, taking a seat on the stylish cream couch while admiring the gorgeous curved hardwood coffee table in front of her. Lucas really was incredibly talented.

"I'll be in the kitchen working on dinner," Janie said. "Let me know if you need anything."

"Please tell me you're making manicotti. I've been craving it for a week now," Bell said.

"I'll see what I can do."

"You're the best, Janie," Bell said.

Janie chuckled as she started to walk back toward the kitchen. "That's what you keep telling me."

"Thanks, Janie," Hope called.

She waved just as she ducked out of the room.

"You know, I really resented Lucas when he told me he was getting me a keeper, but she is a really good cook. If he'd told me he was hiring a personal chef, that conversation would've gone over better." Her eyes crinkled as she laughed. "Getting old sucks, Hope. But having my boy home sure helps."

It was strange how most of the time Bell seemed to be completely lucid and aware of everything that was happening but then periodically slipped in and out of reality. It made Hope feel so much for both Bell and Lucas and what they must be going through. As tough as her relationship with her own mother had been, if Angela kept forgetting details of her life, it would be very disorienting to watch. She wanted to hug Lucas for what he must be going through. And Bell too, for that matter, because she seemed completely aware that her mind was slipping. "I'm glad he's home, too," Hope said quietly.

"He's a good boy, Hope."

"He is," she agreed.

"You still love him, don't you?" Bell asked.

Hope, who'd been taking a sip of the lemonade, choked, and when she was done coughing, she looked at Bell and said, "You don't beat around the bush, do you?"

"I think it's obvious how you feel about each other. Why not speak the truth?"

"Because admitting I love someone to his mother without telling him first just doesn't seem like the right thing to do."

Bell nodded and then tilted her head to the side. "Can I ask you something?"

"Sure."

"Why didn't you move back East with Lucas? Your mom had already left town. I always wondered what was so important to keep you here."

If anyone else had asked her that question, Hope would've bristled. But Bell's tone was full of innocent curiosity. "The first time, I was still in college. The second time, my art gallery had just started to do well. I had a choice to make… stay here and build the business I'd put so much effort into or give it all up to follow a man across the country. I just couldn't."

Bell nodded. "Choices. We all have our reasons. Of course, I'm sure you understand why Lucas felt he had to leave. After everything that happened with his father."

Hope frowned. She'd never met his father. By the time Hope moved to town, he was already out of the picture. Lucas never wanted to talk about him either. He just said that his father had left them and they'd never heard from him again. That was the end of it. "Lucas hasn't told me much about his dad," she admitted. "Only that he left when Lucas was fourteen and never looked back."

Bell nodded. "I'm not surprised. We never talk about him either. There's really nothing to say. Or so I thought. But it turns out I was wrong."

"How so?" Hope leaned forward, realizing that whatever Bell was about to say, it was important for Hope to hear it.

"Lucas's father was a very charismatic guy. When we met, I fell for him very quickly. He's the type of person who can make you feel like you're the center of his universe. It's very intoxicating and not very healthy, but when you're young, it's hard to understand these things. The problem was that, even after I married him, he was making other young women feel the same way."

"Oh. He cheated?" Hope asked, feeling terrible for Bell. She was a warm, lovely woman who deserved so much better.

"Yep. But not only did he not know how to be faithful, he also couldn't hold a job or stick to a budget. While we were married, I often worked three jobs just to keep us from going bankrupt. Looking back, I can't believe I put up with it for so long, but I was and am a believer in vows. And I wanted my son to have a father. What I didn't realize was how badly

Randall was affecting Lucas. I finally hit my tipping point when he started drinking."

Hope winced. It had been worse than she'd thought.

"Randall and Lucas had a good relationship up until the point when Lucas started to understand that his dad never worked, drank too much, and spent too much time with other women. Lucas started to resent that I was working all the time while his father acted the playboy. And when Lucas confronted him about it, Randall told him they were just alike and to stop dreaming of college because he'd never make anything of himself. It was ugly and went on for months before I caught wind of it."

Tears stung Hope's eyes. Lucas didn't deserve that from his father. No child did. And she was beginning to understand why Lucas had been so focused on doing well in school and getting a scholarship. His mother couldn't pay for his education without it. Hope suspected that doing well in life was a big FU to his father, too. "He sounds like he was a very unhappy man."

"That's the truth," Bell agreed. "He didn't like being known as the town drunk and playboy who couldn't hold a job and ultimately took it out on his son. When I learned what was going on, I threw his ass out and told him to never come back. And that's exactly what happened."

"Good for you," Hope said, wiping at her eyes. "I know that couldn't have been easy."

"You know, once I made up my mind, it wasn't so hard. I had Lucas, and he was and always has been my first priority."

Hope suspected Bell wanted her to learn something from the story; she just wasn't sure what. "Bell, why are you telling me this now?"

"Because, sweet girl. I love you, and I'm not sure you understand exactly why he left Premonition Pointe."

"Because he needed to make something of himself. I understand that part. I just don't understand why he couldn't do it here with me. Why was his career so much more important than mine?" There. Hope had finally said the words out loud that she'd been carrying around with her for the past fifteen years.

Bell reached out and cupped Hope's cheek. "It wasn't. He knows that. He left because he needed to prove to himself that he'd never become his father. That he'd make something of himself and not have to rely on his woman to pay the bills. He left Premonition Pointe and the memory of his father, Hope. Not you."

Oh damn. The tears were running unchecked down her cheeks. Why had Bell never told her this before? If she'd known, if she'd realized Lucas had to leave for his own peace of mind, she might have reacted differently. Instead, she'd dug her heels in and remained angry and convinced herself that he'd opted out of the life they'd tried to build together and that her needs hadn't been an important component in their plans. But it had been the opposite. She hadn't realized what he'd needed and supported him. Instead, she'd told him not to call her. She wouldn't do long distance, even though he'd asked her more than once to try.

Hope dropped her head into her hands and let out a deep sigh. "We really messed everything up, didn't we?"

"It's not too late to try again," Bell said softly and sipped at her lemonade.

"No, it's not. You're right about that." Hadn't that been the entire reason Hope had shown up unannounced at his house? She knew she wanted to try again and make this time forever.

Bell blinked, staring at the lemonade glass and then back at Hope. "I thought we were having tea?"

"Janie made us lemonade. It's good," Hope said, holding her glass up.

"Who's Janie?" Bell glanced around, looking confused and a little stressed.

Hope felt panic well in her chest. Clearly, Bell's memory was slipping again. Hope didn't know how to handle it. She decided the best course of action was to remain matter-of-fact and just fill in the details. "She's here to help you around the house while Lucas is at work."

Her frown deepened. "Lucas lives in Boston." Bell glanced around the house, studying all the beautiful details of the restored home. "Wait. Lucas bought us this house. We live here now."

Hope nodded. "Isn't it wonderful? That forest view out the back window is really majestic."

"Lucas told me you always did love this house," she said with a cheeky grin. "Maybe one day you'll move in here with us."

Hope's face warmed, and she knew she was blushing. There wasn't much more she wanted other than to live there with Lucas, his dogs, and Bell, her second mother. "You know, Bell, I think I'd love that."

Bell got up and moved to sit next to Hope on the couch. The older woman gave Hope a big hug and said, "Just tell me when. I'll be ready to help you unpack."

CHAPTER TWENTY-FOUR

*I*t had been twenty-four hours since Hope had left Lucas's house with a new perspective on their past relationship. They both had their reasons for their choices, and it wasn't that they'd chosen their careers over the other person, it was that they'd each chosen *themselves.* Hope because she needed roots and to invest in herself after being abandoned by her mother, and Lucas because he needed to prove he'd never become like his father.

But now? They'd done what they each needed to do, and she was ready to tell him that she was all-in with him. That she was ready to make a commitment to him, whatever that looked like in the future. That they'd make decisions for their life together. It was too bad he'd worked late the night before. It turned out the client he'd gone to see was a few hours away and had a large house that needed *both* cabinets and built-ins. Janie and Bell had both been right. He hadn't gotten in until late and had an early morning meeting scheduled with another client. So even though Hope was giddy and desperate to talk to him, she was holding off on spilling her guts until she could talk to him in person.

She'd spent the morning going over her appointment book, and when she realized her business was down forty percent, she sprang into action, working on how she could win back some of her lost clients. Now she was on her way to talk to Yasmeen. She was going to try to clear the air about the rumors that had caused the woman to cancel her grand opening event. Hope had prepared a proposal that she hoped the owner of the town's new glass gallery couldn't pass up.

Hope parked her car a block away and had to walk through a light drizzle to get to the gallery. She hoped that meant Yasmeen wouldn't be too busy. There weren't a lot of tourists out when it was wet and overcast.

The bell on the door chimed as Hope walked in. The three people at the counter all turned to stare at her. Yasmeen's mouth dropped open, and she shook her head, pointing as if ordering Hope out of her store. But Iris Hartsen, the mayor, didn't see Yasmeen's antics because she was too busy smiling at Hope and waving her over. The third person was one of the men from Gigi's party. Troy something. The photographer if Hope remembered correctly.

"Hope, you're just the person I wanted to see," Iris said. "Come over here. We're brainstorming how to attract more artisan shops to Premonition Pointe."

Part of the mayor's plan for growing the small town was to turn it into an art lover's haven. In addition to the handmade glass shop and a few art galleries, she wanted the downtown to be populated with a few dozen stores all devoted to arts and crafts. She'd ordered an economic development study, and the numbers were in; tourists spent more time and money in the art shops than the tourist trap places that sold mass-produced items that could be ordered from anywhere. The mayor wanted to turn Premonition Pointe into a destination city that had something more to offer than just the beach.

"Uh, okay, but I'm not sure I'm the one to help with that," Hope said.

"You did have an art gallery, didn't you? And your friend Joy is on the board for the Art's Market, right?" the mayor insisted.

"Sure. But I closed my store a while ago, and most of my artists were too busy creating to run their own shops. But I could put some feelers out for you if you'd like," Hope added, wanting to sound helpful. Since the mayor seemed to be ignoring the town gossip, Hope was more than willing to try to give her a hand.

"Hello, Hope. It's nice to see you again," Troy said, holding his hand out. "Skyler can't stop talking about the dog wedding you two are planning. It sounds pretty crazy to me, but that's Sky for you."

Hope smiled at the attractive man, taking in his kind blue eyes and easy smile. "It's one of my more unusual requests, but also one of the most fun. I'm really looking forward to it."

Yasmeen snorted, and when all three of them looked at her, she averted her gaze and said, "Peggy Pitsman is the town's newest up-and-coming event coordinator. If you need to plan an event, she's who I'd call."

So much for winning Yasmeen over, Hope thought.

What a bitch, Troy thought, almost making Hope laugh out loud.

Never in a million years would I book Peggy Pitsman to do anything for me," the mayor thought. *Not even pick up the dog droppings from our yard. That woman is a menace with all her lies and gossip.*

Hope did chuckle to herself then. It was good to know that at least some people in town weren't taking Peggy's words seriously.

"What's so funny, Hope?" Yasmeen demanded. "You do know Peggy's daughter is in the hospital, right?"

"Yes," Hope said, her expression suddenly somber. "It's really terrible. What's that, the fourth overdose this month, Mayor?"

Iris let out a heavy sigh. "It is. I've got a couple deputies working on tracking down leads on where this stuff is coming from, but so far, there's not much to go on. Have any of you heard any rumors we should look into?"

"Nope," Yasmeen said, shaking her head. "The only rumor I heard was the one about Hope trading sexual favors for work."

"Yasmeen!" the mayor admonished. "I already told you that is a vicious lie. Stop being catty."

Hope's eyebrows shot up. She'd never heard the mayor speak to anyone like that, much less a new business owner who'd just opened up shop.

"Sorry." Yasmeen held her hands up. "I thought we'd all heard that one. I didn't say it was true."

The mayor gritted her teeth, and Hope loved her for it. It was nice to have someone on her side for a change. Iris stared at Yasmeen for a long moment and then said, "Try to refrain from being offensive, Yasmeen. It's not a very attractive quality."

The bell chimed again, and the mayor's husband walked

in. He was a shorter man with a thick head of blond hair and a wide smile. "Oh, hello, Iris. Hope. And you, sir, I'm not sure we've met." He held his hand out to Troy, who introduced himself. Then he glanced nervously at Yasmeen. "Hello again."

"Hello, Tom. You're looking good today," she said, giving him a coy smile.

Hope stared at them and frowned. Had Yasmeen really just flirted with the mayor's husband right in front of his wife?

"Looks like you're having a meeting," Tom said to his wife. "What's going on?"

"We're brainstorming ideas for new businesses," she said, looking impatient.

"I know some people," Troy said. "I've got a lot of contacts up and down the coasts in both Southern California and back East. They might be interested in adding another shop here, especially if there's major support from the town."

"Oh, if we're talking about people from out of town, I have a ton of friends already interested," Yasmeen said. "They've been in the art industry for decades. Poppy Tims, Butch Manroe, Annie Deckman. They all have very successful shops."

"What kind of art do they sell?" Iris asked her.

"Oh… um…" She tapped her finger on her chin. "One is into photography, original paintings, that kind of stuff. Butch is all about metal art, both high-end jewelry and wall art. That kind of stuff."

"Huh. That's strange," Troy said.

"Why?" the mayor asked.

He shrugged. "It's just that I know most of the major art galleries down south, and I've never heard of those people."

"Surely you don't know *everyone*," Yasmeen snapped.

"There's no doubt about that. But the art scene is a pretty tightknit circle. I just found that unusual is all." Troy took a step back and shoved his hands in his pockets. "I think I'll take a look around at the art for a minute." He turned to Iris. "Let me know if you want a list of potential contacts."

"I will. Thank you, Troy."

"Anytime." He nodded to Hope. "Good to see you again."

"Thanks, you too." Hope watched as he took a cursory tour around the store and then disappeared back out into the overcast day.

Tom eyed him and the shop and then turned to Yasmeen. "You know, if you need any lumber for new displays, let me know. I'll make you a great deal. I've even got a guy who can build them for you."

"That's kind of you," Yasmeen said and glared at Hope. "The last guy I asked wanted my first born. He had a really bad attitude, too, like he was above helping a fellow business."

Hope turned and rolled her eyes and dropped back to take a look at a shelf of handblown ornaments. She assumed Yasmeen was talking about Lucas. He'd told her about someone who wanted custom shelves but wanted them rushed and at half price. If that was the case, Hope was glad Yasmeen canceled. She didn't need that kind of customer. Keeping an eye on the trio, Hope moved to pretend she was interested in the glassware. While none of their thoughts were coming through, there was a ton of obvious tension between them. And if there was gossip to be had about Yasmeen and the mayor, or the mayor's husband, then Hope was more than willing to eavesdrop the old-fashioned way.

"Don't worry, Yas," Tom said, sliding a hand down her

arm as if to soothe her ruffled feathers. "He was probably just intimidated by all that natural beauty."

"Tom! Seriously?" Iris threw her hands up and stormed out of the store.

"Dammit," Tom mumbled. "I need to go."

Yasmeen reached out and grabbed his wrist. "Wait. She's just being dramatic. Besides, we both know she won't be a problem much longer. Just give it time." She smiled up at him. "Trust me."

He started to lean closer to her but then pulled his hand away. "I need to go. Try to behave for once."

Yasmeen snickered and then disappeared into the back of her store.

Hope was fairly certain they'd forgotten all about her and that Yasmeen was having an affair with the mayor's husband.

Of course she was. The people who yelled the loudest about morality always seemed to be the ones committing the worst sins.

Hope quickly exited the store and spotted Iris and Tom standing under an awning having an argument.

"Don't ever do that to me again!" Iris insisted. "You humiliated me in there."

"I was just being friendly," Tom countered. "You remember friendly, right? It's how civilized people behave."

"Oh, you want to talk about civilized? Let me tell you what civilized is. It means supporting your wife instead of trying to exploit every single business connection I have for your own gain. It's unethical for you to use my office, my title, and the trust I've gained from this community just to add more accounts to your roster."

Hope frowned. Tom owned a lumber business. Why was

4

4

Iris so upset about him working with Lucas? The man needed a supplier.

"I didn't use your connections! How is Lucas King one of your connections?" he demanded. His cheeks were so red he looked like she'd just slapped him.

"Because he came to me for help with zoning, and now it looks like I did him favors just so you could get his business. What the hell, Tom? You know how this all works. We need to be so far above board that we don't even need a life vest. Don't you see that?"

He glanced at the shop and spotted Hope lurking there. She stared at her phone, trying to pretend she was waiting for an Uber.

Finally, he turned his attention back to the mayor. "I'll do what I want. That's what you do." Then he strode away, leaving the mayor shaking with anger.

Hope wanted to go to her to offer comfort, but she took off too quickly, and Hope suspected she was the type of woman who burned off her frustrations by working, not by gossiping with girlfriends. But she'd run the idea by Grace, Joy, and Gigi and see if they were open to inviting Iris to a coven meeting if the opportunity arose. She quite liked the mayor.

"Oh. Em. Gee. Did you just witness all of that?" Skyler asked. He was holding Pete's hand as they walked down the sidewalk toward Hope, and they had takeout bags from Abalone. "Talk about entertainment. Do you know what they were arguing about?"

"Sky," Pete said with a chuckle as he shook his head.

"Oh, come on, Petey. Hope had a front row seat to the show. She needs to spill because she's my new bestie."

Hope laughed. "Well, if you must know, I personally

witnessed her husband flirting with Yasmeen. When Iris stalked off, Yasmeen told her husband to not worry so much because Iris wouldn't be a problem much longer. I think they are having an affair."

"That is scandalous," Skyler said, putting one hand over his chest as he craned his neck to the side.

"An affair?" Pete asked, frowning. "I don't think that's it. Or at least not all of it. They could be messing around, but if they are, I'd rather not think about it." He shuddered as if he'd be scarred just thinking about them together.

"Then what else could it be?" Hope asked.

Pete pursed his lips and cast a glance at the store behind them. "It's because she just filed today to run against the mayor in the next election."

Both Hope and Skyler let out a loud gasp and then said, "Nooooo."

CHAPTER TWENTY-FIVE

*H*ope was exhausted by the time she walked into her house. After the scene at Yasmeen's glass shop, she'd gotten a call from Troy. He was planning to throw a dinner party for some of his artist friends who were coming to town in a few weeks and asked for her help. She'd been glad to get her mind off the scene back at Yasmeen's shop. Who knew a small town could be full of so much drama? Wasn't there already enough going on without the added bonus of Yasmeen trying to run for mayor? Hope feared that if she managed to get enough of her gossiping friends to vote for her, the town was doomed.

The house was dark and entirely too quiet. Her mother's car was out front, but there was no sign of her in the house. "Mom?" Hope called, dropping the mail on a side table.

"I'm here," her mother called from down the hallway. A light flipped on, and Angela appeared wearing yoga pants and a wrinkled sweatshirt. Her dark hair was a mess, and there was a pillow wrinkle creased on her face.

"Did you have a nice nap?" Hope asked, suddenly

intensely jealous. How nice it would've been to sleep the afternoon away.

She nodded and wiped the sleep out of her eyes. "I was starting to get a migraine. The nap helped."

Hope grimaced. "I'm sorry. Has it gone away, or do you need some medication?" Her mother had suffered from migraines off and on when Hope was a kid, but they'd gotten much worse during the last year before she'd taken off and left Hope on her own. "Is it worsened by all the telepathy?"

"These days, yes. When I get overloaded with other people's thoughts, it takes a toll." She ran a hand down her face and yawned. "I passed out."

Hope took a seat in her oversized chair and studied her mother. "Where were you that you got overwhelmed?"

"Pointe of View Café. I was listening in on a conversation between two college-age guys. They were delivery drivers who were talking about their jobs, but one of them was thinking about some extra packages he delivers on the side. How he didn't want to do it anymore after all the overdoses, but that *she* would kill him if he tried to quit."

Holy shit. Hope leaned forward, suddenly very interested in what her mother had to say. All week her mom had been spending some time listening in on people, but there hadn't been anything of interest. Now it appeared she'd stumbled on a jackpot and run into a guy who was transporting ashe. "*She* would kill him? The person we're looking for is a she?"

"That's what it sounded like to me," she said with a nod. "He thought about the time he smoked some and was frightened about how he couldn't really remember anything. Right about that time, I got up and went over to them, intending to get a name. I pretended I thought he was the son of a family friend and called him Hal when I said hello.

But the little bastard thought it was funny and just went with it."

"Funny guy," Hope said dryly. "His friend didn't think about his name or anything, did he?"

"Nope. He did call him E, so that's something to go on I guess, but it's really frustrating that I don't seem to be getting anywhere on this."

"Mom," Hope said, getting up and moving to sit with her. "You've been fantastic. Now I know I'm looking for a woman, and if a delivery driver who goes by E or has a name that starts with E shows up, we'll know to check him out." She threw her arms around Angela and gave her a hug. "I'm sorry listening in on people's thoughts has been so hard on you. Want me to make some dinner? Or tea or something?"

Angela shook her head. "No, thanks. I'm actually going to go out for a walk and get some fresh air on the beach. I could use some space from people."

Hope knew that meant she just wanted to quiet her mind, and even though Hope was the only other person in the house, it wasn't as if her mom could turn off her ability to hear her thoughts.

"That's right, bunny. I'm craving some peace." Angela kissed her on the cheek and rose from the couch, disappearing down the hall. A few minutes later, while Hope was in the kitchen warming some leftover pasta, she heard the front door open and then shut.

She'd just sat down at her table when the door opened and closed again. Footsteps sounded on the hardwood floors, making Hope frown. "Did you forget something?"

"Nope," Lucas said from the kitchen doorway. "I remember *everything*."

Hope turned and smiled at him as her heart sped up.

Damn, she'd missed him, and it had only been forty-eight hours since she'd last seen him. "You're a sight for sore eyes. I didn't know you were coming by tonight."

Lucas crossed the kitchen and wrapped her in his arms. Without a word, he covered her mouth with his and kissed her slowly, taking his time to explore her lips, tongue, mouth. By the time he pulled back, she was breathless and leaning into him, wanting more.

"I went by your house to see you yesterday," Hope said.

"I know. My mom really enjoyed the visit." He brushed a lock of her dark hair behind her ear.

"She said you were working."

"Yeah. I was doing a job estimate. I'm sorry I missed you." He cupped his hand around the back of her neck and pulled her in for another kiss, this time gently tugging on her bottom lip, making her entire body tingle.

Hope closed her eyes and let out a tiny moan. Damn, it felt good to be in his arms again.

"I want you, Hope," he said huskily, moving his mouth to her neck and trailing kisses down to her shoulder.

"That's—ah!" He'd chosen that moment to sink his teeth into flesh, making it sting slightly. "That's not fair," she breathed. "You know that always gets me going."

"No one said I was going to be fair." He brought his hands to her sides and started to tug at her shirt.

She chuckled. "This is going to sound silly, since I'm a grown-ass woman, but my mom could come home at any time."

He immediately lifted his head and stared into her eyes. "No she won't. On my way in, she told me she'd be scarce and to get in here and show you just how much I want you."

Hope narrowed her eyes at him. "She did *not* say that."

"Oh, she did. In fact, she told me that she was going to go check into a hotel so that we'd have our privacy." He took the opportunity to tug her closer to him so that she was pressed against his fit body.

"You're messing with me, right?" She grinned up at him, loving their exchange. It was light and playful, just like it had been before. She'd always loved making love with him. Their nights had been full of laughter, and sex with him was just fun.

He chuckled. "I know it sounds like it, but she really did say that. I'm pretty sure it's because all I've been thinking about since I kissed you last is how much I want to trail my tongue over every inch of your skin."

Hope groaned. "She read your thoughts, ordered you to pleasure me, and then decided to get a hotel room? This is very surreal."

"It is, but I'm not complaining. I just want you." He ran a light thumb over her lips.

As much as she wanted to drag him off to her bedroom right at that moment, she still had things to say and didn't want to do it in a post-sex haze. Hope took a step back and cleared her throat. "I think it's obvious I want this as much as you do, but we need to talk first."

Lucas dropped his hand and stiffened. "That sounds ominous."

Hope chuckled softly. "It's not. At least I don't think it is." She took him by the hand and led him into the living room. After gently pushing him down into the oversized chair, she climbed onto his lap, letting her legs drape over one of the arms.

"This could be worse." He wrapped his arms around her and nuzzled her neck.

Hope twined her fingers in his and said, "I owe you an apology."

Lucas stopped kissing her jawline and pulled back to look at her. "For what?"

"For blaming everything on you when you left fifteen years ago."

His eyes narrowed slightly and searched hers. "But I was the one who left after we decided to try to build something here."

"I know. But what I like to conveniently forget is that you asked me repeatedly to go with you and I refused. Honestly, Lucas, I didn't even consider it." She felt her cheeks heat, and she had to avert her gaze just to regain her composure. Maybe it hadn't been such a good idea to sit on his lap while talking. She'd wanted them to be close, physically connected when she declared her love for him. But admitting her own faults while being unable to retreat was harder than she expected.

"You didn't even consider it?" he asked then thought, *did she even love me the way I loved her?*

"Of course I loved you," she blurted and immediately regretted it. Her ability to read minds was a complete menace, and if she were in his shoes, she'd very much regret him being able to look into her mind. "Sorry. I can't help it when thoughts come through."

His lips quirked up, and he gave her a gentle kiss. "It's all right. I know you're not doing it on purpose. I guess that will keep me honest."

"You're always honest." That was one thing she knew all the way in her bones. They'd had a lot of issues in the past, but trust had never been one of them.

"I like to think so." He squeezed her hand and added,

"Now, I'm interested in hearing why you never even considered moving back East with me." His tone was more curious than accusatory and, not for the first time, she found herself in awe of this man. If he were the one telling her he'd never considered staying in Premonition Pointe, she'd have been crushed.

"It's not that I didn't consider it. I probably did, briefly. It's just that I didn't *seriously* consider it. I knew right away I wasn't going. I had my gallery, and you'd already left me once. I was independent, and you know that was important to me. I wasn't ready to give up my entire life to chase you around the country. Especially when I was the one who had to give up everything."

"You're saying the gallery and your independence was more important than us?" he asked. This time there was some pain etched in his expression.

Hope reached up and smoothed the lines between his eyes. "No. They weren't. That's what I've come to realize. But what *was* more important was me. Because of my past trauma of being left by the two people I loved most, I had to put my own needs first, and unconsciously I did that."

He stared at her, waiting for her to continue. There was no judgement rolling off him, and it was that more than anything else that encouraged her to continue.

"I needed roots, Lucas. A home. A support system. Ties to my mom and stability. Premonition Pointe gave me all of those things. My coven, my gallery, my home, the possibility that my mom would show up and I'd have a family again."

"I could've given you stability," he said quietly.

She shook her head. "Not the kind I needed. Not back then, anyway. It took me a long time to realize why I didn't run off to Boston with you. My gut just wouldn't let me, and

I think for a while I thought that was a sign that I shouldn't be with you. But the truth is, I have huge abandonment issues, and it was impossible for me to run off to an uncertain world where I had to depend on someone else. Don't you see? I had to make something of myself here, just like you had to make something of yourself somewhere else. I didn't go because of *me*. Not because of you. It's important you understand that."

His hold tightened around her and he buried his face in her neck.

She let him hold her like that and barely breathed while she waited for him to say something.

Finally, he lifted his head and kissed her temple. "I wanted to stay with you, baby. I really did."

"I know," she said softly.

"You do?"

She smiled up at him. "My conversation with your mom was really enlightening. It turns out we both had something to prove. We just had to go about it two different ways. I know why you left. And I even understand it. Staying here wasn't in the cards for you. Just as leaving wasn't for me."

"I've always loved you. You know that, right?"

"Yes," she said, not even caring that her eyes stung with tears. "I've always loved you, too. There's never been anyone else who's had my heart."

He moved his hand to cover the left side of her chest, and her heart sped up under the weight of it. "Same here. I'm home now, Hope. Do you think we can finally put everything behind us and start again?"

"I'd love nothing more than that," she said with a shaky laugh. "The question is, what happens in the future? Are we a couple who moves through life together, or are we both still so independent that we'll never compromise when it comes to our careers?"

"I can compromise," he said quickly. "I've moved home for my mom. But I'd be lying if I said I hadn't thought about coming back for you for the last fourteen years. That first year in Boston, I was too hurt. But then I started to miss you, and…" He shrugged. "I'm here now, and I'm not leaving. Not ever."

"What if I get a job in Boston? Or down South? Or in Europe? Will you come with me?" she asked, even though those scenarios were highly unlikely. Her coven was in Premonition Pointe. So was her entire life. She didn't want to leave. She knew that about herself. Still, she wanted to hear his answer.

"If my mom is taken care of, then yes. I'm going where you go." His conviction was off the charts, and it warmed her from head to toe.

"Lucas," she said, turning and taking his face with both hands. "I love you. I've always loved you. I want to be with you forever."

"I want that, too," he said, staring at her intently.

"Good. Do you think we can make a promise to each other that if one of us has an opportunity outside of this town we will make the decision together on what's best for both of us? For our life together instead of what's better for you or for me?"

"You mean like a team?" he asked, his eyes crinkling with joy.

"Yes. If we're going to live the rest of our lives together, then let's do just that. I've planted my roots and you've made yourself into a very successful businessman. Let's figure out what's next together."

"Deal." He stood in one fluid motion, still holding her in his arms. Hope let out a gasp of surprise and held on tighter. "I think what's next is a trip to your bedroom," Lucas said, his voice husky with need. "What do you say?"

"Yes," she said and kissed him on the lips. "Definitely, yes."

CHAPTER TWENTY-SIX

*H*ope moved through her day with a permanent smile on her face. Her evening with Lucas had been nothing short of magical. She could still feel his touch on her skin, his soft lips, and his warmth as he held her all night. She'd never been a snuggler, not even when they were together before. But this time around, it was as if they needed to make up for all the years they hadn't held onto each other.

If that wasn't enough, she'd woken to fresh coffee and egg croissants. Who knew that when Lucas had run off to the East Coast he'd learned to cook? They had a leisurely morning and then made plans for that evening after they were both done with catching up on some work.

Nothing was going to ruin her good mood. Not even her mother, who was currently making comments about everything that ran through Hope's head. She'd tried to clamp down on the memories, but some kept popping up at the least opportune times. Like when she'd walked into the kitchen to grab a fresh cup of coffee and remembered exploring every inch of Lucas's body the night before.

"Just make sure he reciprocates, bunny. Oral sex should be a two-way street," Angela said without looking up from the newspaper she held in her hands.

"*Mother!* Please. If you can't stay out of my head, at least keep your commentary to yourself," Hope groused, trying to make her mind blank.

"I'm just saying. Women have needs, too." She smiled at Hope. "I'm glad you had a good time last night. Does this mean I might get a son-in-law someday soon?"

"Ohmigod," Hope said, rolling her eyes. She shoved a cookie in her mouth and ignored her mother's question. As Hope made her way back down the hall, she heard her mother snickering to herself. "You're going to pay for that," Hope called and then closed herself up in her home office.

* * *

"I DON'T THINK we're going to find dogwoods," Skyler said, eyeing the potted trees at the nursery. Hope had met up with him in the afternoon to discuss the flowers and greenery they were going to use at the dog wedding.

Hope had already told him they were a longshot unless he wanted to order them online and have them shipped. "They don't bloom in the fall anyway. Don't you want something that has flowers?"

"Yeah," he said with a sigh. "I just really liked the idea of dogwoods for the dogs."

"I don't think we need to be so on the nose," Hope said with a laugh. "What do you think about sunflowers? We can do a photoshoot of them running through a field and then have them at the ceremony. Sunflowers are just so happy; they seem right for the occasion."

He pursed his lips and then nodded slowly. "I could get on board with sunflowers. They're—"

Hope's phone rang, cutting him off. "Just a sec," she said to Skyler, recognizing the ringtone she'd picked for Jackson. "Hey, what's up?" she said into the phone.

"There's been another overdose," he said, his voice low as if he were whispering into the phone. "This time it was our delivery driver. He was rolling in our weekly supply of cups when he just passed out in the back room."

"Delivery driver?" Hope asked, remembering what her mother had said the day before. "Is he still there, or did the paramedics take him already?"

"No paramedics, and yes, he's still here. It wasn't as bad as Whitley's episode or Spencer's. He came out of the seizure pretty quickly and even knocked my phone out of my hand when he realized I was calling for help. He's terrified of being forced to talk to the authorities, but I think he wants to tell someone what's going on. He seems nervous, but he's in no hurry to leave."

"I'll be right there," she said and hung up.

"You're leaving me?" Skyler asked, blinking at her in disbelief. "But how will I know when I've gone completely off the rails?"

She reached over and gave him a quick hug. "I'm sorry. It's an emergency. Just don't buy anything today. Take pictures of what you like, and we'll go over them together, okay?"

"Not buy anything?" he asked with a laugh and then winked at her. "Good one." He sobered then as if remembering that she'd just told him she had an emergency. "I hope everything is okay. Talk to you tomorrow?"

"Definitely." She blew him a kiss and took off.

* * *

ETHAN POMEROY SAT in the back room of Pointe of View Café with his back pressed against the wall, sipping a cup of water. He wore black faded jeans and a white polo shirt that had a *Seaside Delivers* logo stitched near the collar. Hope eyed him, wondering what she could say to get him talking. Jackson had read the guy right. He definitely did not want to leave. But he didn't seem to be interested in talking either.

Hope sat down right next to him and said, "Rough day?"

"You have no idea," he spat out and then started coughing. "My boss is a bitch, and because of her, I almost died today."

"Almost, but you didn't," Hope said, trying to sound reassuring.

He snorted. "No thanks to her. If I'd taken as big of a hit as she required, then I probably would be in a coma right about now. I can't keep doing this. Either she'll kill me, or the drugs will."

"Who's she?" Hope asked.

He jerked his head in her direction. "My boss. Who else would it be?"

Hope shrugged. "No idea. Are you talking about your boss at Seaside Delivers?"

Ethan glanced around and then shook his head slowly. "I mean my boss, the one who controls everything I do with that damned drug."

"She forces you to take it?" Hope tried again.

He stared at the floor for a long moment, and just when

Hope was convinced he wasn't going to answer, he nodded. "Before and after every shift. It's to keep us addicted to it so that we'll keep her secrets."

"That's brutal, Ethan. If you don't mind me asking, how did you get involved in this?"

He picked up a piece of coffee cake that Jackson had left for him and started to crumble it into pieces. "It was through my delivery job, actually. It was only my second day when my supervisor told me to make a special delivery. It was for an extra hundred bucks, so I did it and ended up at this fancy house in the hills. The woman who opened the door was really sweet and invited me inside to this swank-ass party. Damn, it was cool. Champagne, gorgeous views, gorgeous women, and plenty of drugs." He shook his head sadly. "I was so naïve."

"We all are sometimes," Hope said, hoping to keep him talking. "Something happened that night. What was it?"

He closed his eyes tightly and shook his head. Hope had the distinct impression he was trying to dislodge the memory from his brain. But then suddenly, he opened his eyes and looked right at her. "A girl overdosed that night. She didn't make it. Oh, god. She didn't make it," he said with a sob, covering his mouth with one hand and doubling over to rock back and forth. "That girl died, and when I freaked out, demanding that the paramedics be called, I was told that I was the one who supplied her and the rest of the party with ashe, and if any authorities were called, I'd be the one getting arrested."

It was Hope's turn to blink at him. "They pinned the drugs on you?"

He shook his head. "No need to. I was the one who delivered the drugs. Only I had no idea what was in that package." Ethan slumped forward and said in a quiet voice, "I wanted nothing to do with any of that, but when I tried to leave that night, they cornered me. Told me they had it all on video. That's when they threatened me. I could either work for them or go to jail for trafficking drugs and possibly even manslaughter. They didn't leave me a choice. Now I'm out there picking up the product from the supplier, delivering it to the pushers, and being forced into addiction so I won't care what they do as long as I get my hit."

Hope wanted to tuck the kid into her pocket and take him home to keep him safe. He couldn't be older than nineteen, and somehow, he'd managed to get leveraged into a major drug trafficking scheme. "What would you say if I said I could help you?"

"You can't. Trust me on this," he said, leaning forward and resting his forehead on his knees.

Hope stifled a sigh. Of course, she could help him, but what would that mean for Ethan? It certainly sounded like the people controlling him were ruthless. Getting him to open up was going to be hard. She could see that he was terrified about being caught up in a drug ring but also terrified that if he didn't say something things were only going to get worse. "You said you pick up the drugs from the supplier. Can you give me a hint of who that might be? Then I can investigate and leave you out of it."

He shook his head, but Hope was ready for him. She opened her mind and studied him, waiting for his thoughts to seep in.

"I can't tell you," he muttered over and over again, leaving her tired from trying to listen in on his almost nonexistent inner thoughts.

"Okay." Hope stood and held out a business card. "If you

ever want to be the hero, all you have to do is call this number. I'll be ready to listen. I swear."

He stared at her card, and then just like that, his thoughts poured into her mind. Everything was a jumble at first. The voices overwhelmed her, and once again, she felt both admiration and pity for her mother. Hope could not do that all the time.

Some of the clutter in Ethan's mind had vanished, and a scene at Lucas's shop started to play in his head. It was Lucas spraying his sawdust with some sort of liquid treatment, and then a few days later, Ethan picked it up and delivered it to a warehouse where workers were waiting to process the sawdust.

The scene shifted to them turning the sawdust into small pellets that were then sent off into the world as party favors.

Hope sat frozen next to him, her mouth dry, and she felt as if she was going to pass out. That scene had started at Lucas's shop and had shown him treating his sawdust with some unknown substance.

Ashe. It had to be.

Which meant the man she loved was the supplier for ashe.

"I'm going to be sick," she said and rushed to the bathroom.

CHAPTER TWENTY-SEVEN

"*H*ope? Are you all right?" Jackson called through the door of the bathroom.

She was standing at the sink, splashing water on her face. After connecting Lucas to the drug ashe, she'd lost the contents of her stomach, and her thoughts were whirling. How was it possible that Lucas was involved with distributing drugs? The man had never taken them himself. Was it a money issue? Did he need the cash to take care of his mom?

That didn't make sense either. She'd recently retired from the school district and had plenty of benefits through the state.

"Hope?" Jackson tried again. "If you don't answer me, I'm going to kick the door in."

She flicked the lock on the door and pulled it open. His expression was haggard, and he looked like he'd aged ten years in ten minutes. Hope glanced in the mirror, winced at her pale skin and the dark circles under her eyes, and decided he looked better than she did.

Jackson slipped into the bathroom and leaned against the closed door. "Do you need anything? Ginger ale? Or maybe some saltine crackers?"

She smiled weakly at him. "That's sweet of you, but I think what I really need are answers." She needed to talk to Lucas.

"I think I know a way we can make that happen," Jackson said.

"How's that?"

"One of the girls who overdosed a few weeks ago told me she'd be willing to meet me to talk. I texted her a few minutes ago, letting her know there was another incident. She said she'd meet us at Beachside Beer Garden in a few minutes. I thought if we got her together with Ethan, that maybe they'd be willing to talk more. You know, strength in numbers?"

Hope nodded. "That's a good idea. Besides, it can't hurt. Give me just a sec, and I'll be right out."

He nodded and disappeared.

There were some other people she needed for this rendezvous. Hope pulled her phone out of her pocket and sent a text to her mother. Then she sent a group text to her coven. If Lucas really was involved, she was going to need her girls. The only person she didn't text was Lucas. She just couldn't wrap her head around the idea that he was the one they'd been looking for this whole time. How was that even possible? She'd told him about the person wanting to use his business to move drugs, and he'd dismissed that idea so easily and with so much conviction that she'd never believed that he would be involved.

There was also the fact that she'd never heard one thought from him about drugs. But then, she rarely heard his thoughts at all. Was he that good at concealing what was going on in his head? Her chest tightened, making it hard to breathe. She pressed her palm over her breastbone and prayed she wasn't having a heart attack.

* * *

HOPE WAITED with Ethan out in front of Pointe of View Café while Jackson clocked out from his shift. She was still feeling nauseated, but whatever was going on with her was nothing compared to Ethan. The poor man was sweating up a storm while complaining of being cold as if he had a fever.

"Hey, do we need to take you to the urgent care?" Hope asked him. "You don't look well."

"I'm fine," he said, closing his eyes and giving her a pained look. "This always happens. It will pass."

"Always? How many times have you overdosed on that stuff?" She couldn't help asking, even though she knew she should wait until she had backup.

"This is the third time." He coughed, and Hope was ready to stuff him in her car and take him home where she could tuck him under a blanket and ply him with tea and cinnamon toast until he felt better.

"Were all of them forced on you?" she asked.

He nodded.

"That's horrific, Ethan. You have to stop delivering for... this person."

"I can't," he said in a whisper so low that she barely heard him. "She'll kill me."

"Ready?" Jackson asked as he walked out the door.

"I guess so." Ethan shoved his hands in his pockets and hunched his shoulders.

They started to walk the two blocks to the Beachside Beer Garden where they were meeting Riley, Jackson's contact. They were all quiet, lost in their own thoughts. Hope heard Ethan praying that he was doing the right thing, and she heard Jackson praying that he never had to witness another overdose. Hope prayed that her mother and her coven would get to the Beer Garden before she did so that they'd be around if she needed them. Her mother was the most important. She wanted her mom to listen in. Her friends were needed for when they were ready to go kick some ass.

The Beer Garden wasn't busy. Considering it was still early in the afternoon, that wasn't a surprise, and it made it the perfect place to meet. They could sit outside and have a certain amount of privacy. But not much considering Angela was there.

Hope spotted her mom sitting at a table with Grace out on the patio. It looked as if Gigi and Joy hadn't arrived yet. That was okay. As long as Angela was there.

Jackson led the way to a table closest to the beach where a petite blonde sat, picking at a bucket of French fries. "Hey, Riley," he said. "How are you doing? Better?"

She stared at Ethan, her expression a little panicked.

"It's okay. This is Ethan. Remember I told you I was bringing someone who went through the same thing," Jackson said.

"I remember." She swallowed and glanced away so that she wasn't looking at him. "That's how I looked for days after I... Well, the recovery was awful. I still get the shakes."

Ethan nodded. "Yeah. That happens."

Both of the young people were quiet as the waiter came to take their orders. They all requested water, so Grace put

240

in an order of nachos just so the waiter wasn't wasting his time. When he was gone, Hope turned to Riley and introduced herself. "I'm really glad to meet you, Riley."

The young woman let out a grunt that Hope didn't know how to interpret.

"Um, okay. So, can you tell us where you got your ashe? Or more specifically from who?" Hope asked.

"Why? Do you need a hookup?" she barked back, narrowing her eyes at Hope.

"Riley," Jackson said with a sigh. "I thought you wanted to help us bring down the people who did this to you."

"Not people. Person," she said and stared at Hope with a look of disgust. "Like she doesn't know already. Right, Hope?"

Hope frowned, trying to read the woman's thoughts, but the only thing that came through was the word *bitch*. *Okay, then*, Hope thought. How had she possibly rubbed this woman the wrong way already? "I don't know what you're talking about."

"Sure you do. Are you and your boyfriend in on this together? Is this your way of reminding me to keep my mouth shut?"

"I really don't know—"

Ethan jerked in the seat next to her and sucked in a sharp breath.

Hope followed his gaze and spotted Yasmeen and Peggy Pitsman being seated on the other side of the patio.

"Ethan," Riley hissed. "Keep it together."

He shook his head and stood up. "I can't do this. I have to go." Before anyone could stop him, he ran out onto the beach, heading in the direction of the pier.

"What the heck was that all about?" Hope asked.

"He's afraid if he talks you're going to end him," Riley said.

"Me?" Hope jerked back, shocked. "Why would I do something like that? I'm trying to help him."

"Stop playing dumb. Everyone knows you're the lady supplying ashe," she yelled as she stood, and then she turned and snarled at Jackson. "I don't know what game you're playing here, but I'm out. I don't want anything to do with your dangerous drug. You hear me? Now stay the hell away from me and my friends." She turned and started to stride toward the door that led inside.

"What the hell was that—" Hope started, but then she abruptly stopped when she saw Yasmeen give Riley the tiniest nod.

Suddenly she felt an eerie calm settle over her. She'd been set up. Clearly, Riley was trying to pin the drugs on her, but what she didn't understand was why? Hope glanced at Peggy and Yasmeen. Both of them had their eyes narrowed in her direction. Then Peggy jumped out of her chair and came charging toward Hope.

Hope stood, holding her hands up in a stop motion, but Peggy used both hands and pushed her back, sending her stumbling into their table. It crashed to the ground and beer splattered everywhere.

"You! It's your fault my daughter almost died." Peggy pushed her again. "I knew you were trouble. Just knew it. And then you dared to tell me to print a retraction about your business practices, all while promising to find out who supplied my daughter with drugs. You're despicable. Pure trash. Someone call the cops. This bitch needs to be locked up before I bury her."

"Hey," Jackson said, trying to squeeze between them.

"That's enough. Peggy calm down. Hope doesn't have anything to do with those drugs, and you know it."

"No. You heard that girl. She called her out right in front of everyone, and Hope didn't even deny it. She's still not denying it even though I'm screaming at her."

Hope was too busy watching Yasmeen. The woman was tapping furiously on her phone and thinking, *One down. One more to go.*

Was that a calculated take down? Was Yasmeen behind all of this? Or was she just trying to make Hope's life hell? She glanced at her mother, who was also staring at Yasmeen, her expression intense as if she were concentrating.

She turned her attention back to Peggy, who was crying now and still accusing Hope of trying to kill her daughter.

"Peggy, there are no circumstances that I would ever even use a drug like ashe, much less produce and sell it. I don't know why Riley thought that about me, but I can assure you, it's one hundred percent untrue."

"I don't believe you," she snapped.

"I'm sorry to hear that." Hope started to move toward Yasmeen, intent on confronting her, but stopped in her tracks when she heard Joy frantically call her name.

"Hope!" Joy appeared on the patio with Gigi in tow. "We have to go. Now. It's Lucas. He's being arrested."

CHAPTER TWENTY-EIGHT

$\mathscr{H}$ ope's heart stopped when she heard Joy's words. "Arrested?" she breathed. "Why?"

"He's being charged with possession with intent to distribute ashe. The cops just picked him up and have a warrant to search his premises." Joy tugged on her arm. "We have to go get him a lawyer. Come on."

Hope was frozen in her tracks. She hadn't really believed it when she'd learned he might be involved. She'd thought that there had to be some mistake. Lucas was not a person who broke the law or did drugs.

But it's been fifteen years since you knew him that well, she told herself. Her stomach rolled again.

"Just as I thought," Yasmeen said. "Looks like you and your boyfriend both deserve to be locked up. Thank the gods I didn't hire you. Who knows what kind of trash you'd have invited to my opening?" She shoved her phone into her back pocket and said, "Peggy, let's go. We have better things to do than share space with this criminal."

Yasmeen shoved past Hope, nearly knocking her down,

but was stopped in her tracks when Angela stepped in front of her.

"You have some nerve," Angela growled at her. "How dare you try to pin this on my daughter and Lucas? You thought you'd masterminded this whole thing by setting up someone else to take the fall for your deadly drugs. You even targeted the mayor's husband and blackmailed him to help you after you set him up, making it that much easier to take her job and then turn Premonition Pointe into your own drug capital. Well, guess what, bitch. I'm the one who's standing in your way now. You won't get away with this."

Yasmeen glared at her. "Crazy, just like your daughter. Maybe you two can get a buy one, get one free at the mental health clinic."

Hope kept her steady gaze on her mother. She knew all the way down to her bones that Angela had heard Yasmeen thinking about everything she'd done to wreak havoc on the town. It was all true. Which meant Lucas wasn't involved. Relief rushed through her, and the tension freezing her in place started to dissipate.

"Hope?" Joy tried again. "We need to go. Lucas has been arrested."

Hope started to move toward her but was nearly knocked down as Peggy Pitsman suddenly shot by her and tackled Yasmeen, who was trying to leave the Beer Garden.

"You bitch!" Peggy screamed as she yanked at Yasmeen's hair. "You did this to my daughter, and you're going to pay!"

Yasmeen let out a cry and elbowed Peggy in the ribs. When Peggy's hold loosened, Yasmeen rolled and scrambled to her feet. "Peggy! You don't really believe these lies, do you? I'm your friend. I would never—"

Peggy hauled off and slapped her. Hard. "Angela is

telepathic. A powerful one. I guess you didn't know that. Now we all know how awful you are. A person who makes money by giving drugs to kids—oomph!"

Yasmeen gut-punched her, and the pair of them crashed to the ground again, rolling around, knocking tables and chairs over.

Hope stared at them with disgust and then walked over to Joy. "Let's go. We need to figure out what to do about Lucas."

"I'm coming. I have the details that should clear his name," Angela said, clutching Hope's arm.

Hope gave her mother a grateful smile and nodded. "Thanks, Mom. Without you here..." She shook her head. "I don't even want to think about it."

"You don't have to. I've got your back, bunny." She squeezed Hope's hand. "Now come on. Let's go get your man."

"I'll stay here and make sure the police get statements from everyone. I've already called them," Grace said.

Gigi nodded. "I'll stay, too."

"Thank you," Hope said and glanced at Jackson. "What about you? Do you want to come with us or...?"

He shook his head. "I'm going to go find Ethan. I think he genuinely wanted to tell us what was happening but lost his nerve when Riley was spewing her crap."

"Yeah. I think so too." Hope turned to Angela. "Yasmeen put her up to that, didn't she?"

Her mom nodded. "Yes. Yasmeen got wind that you and Jackson were investigating, and she decided to have a couple of people on her payroll help to set you up. The plan was to have Lucas arrested and then pin you as his co-conspirator. Riley was all in. Ethan doesn't want anything to do with any of it. He was only here because Yasmeen threatened him and his family."

That's what Hope suspected. She met Jackson's gaze. "Go find him. He obviously needs a friend right now. If you can get him to come make a statement, I'm sure it will go a long way to keep him from getting swept up in the fallout of this."

"I'm on it." Jackson took off down the beach toward the pier.

Hope glanced one more time at the two women still wrestling on the patio and then strode out of the Beer Garden, intent on freeing her man.

* * *

HOPE SAT with Angela in an interrogation room, fuming. They'd been at the police station for no less than five hours, and still, no one had taken the time to talk to them. In fact, it had damned near taken a miracle to even get into the room. When they arrived, they'd inquired about bailing Lucas out. But his bail hadn't been set yet, and they had to wait. Then they'd tried to give a statement about everything they knew and were brushed off.

Hope had been pacing the police station, anxious about not being able to do something, while Joy kept them supplied with vending machine snacks. Angela had a much better plan. She started reciting everything the cop at the front desk was thinking. Even when he was thinking about how much he wanted to go home and give himself a home pedicure.

By the time Angela revealed that he had a crush on one of his coworkers and desperately wanted to paint her toenails, he'd been bright red and frantic to get rid of them. That's when Hope and Angela been moved to the interrogation room. Joy was left to wait for them out front. Hope just didn't know if the lead investigator was ever going to talk to them.

"Maybe I should start telling all their secrets," Angela said. "That one over there dyes his hair."

"I don't really think that's an embarrassing thing that anyone will care about, Mom," Hope said.

"His pubic hair, Hope."

Hope couldn't help it. She snorted and gasped out, "But why?"

"He doesn't want to look old when he drops his drawers. Everyone loves a silver fox until his snake is laying in the gray patch."

Hope just stared at her and rolled her eyes. "That was bad."

Angela laughed. "So? You were distracted for a few moments, right?"

There was a knock on the window, startling them, and then the mayor walked in and took a seat. "Hello, Hope. Angela. I hear you're waiting to give a statement about what went down today at the Beachside Beer Garden."

Hope sat up straight and placed her hands on the table. "Lucas had no idea he was involved with ashe. He was set up."

Iris Hartsen sat across from them and nodded. "I know."

"You do?" Hope asked. "Then why was he arrested?"

"The detectives weren't privy to all the information we've been collecting over these last few weeks. It was a… sensitive matter," Iris said.

Hope turned to her mother and was surprised to see her lips curve into a grin. "Mom, what aren't you two telling me?"

"You're a sneaky one, Mayor," Angela said.

Iris smiled back at Angela. "By now, Tom should've known that I was three steps ahead of him this whole time. My only regret is that we didn't have the evidence sooner to bring down the drug ring. Far too many people were hurt because ashe was distributed around town."

"Okay, someone needs to fill me in here," Hope exclaimed, throwing her hands up in the air. "You knew that Yasmeen was the drug boss and that your husband was involved?"

The mayor nodded. "When Tom started working with her, I didn't know exactly what was going on, but I knew something was up."

Hope raised her eyebrows. "You didn't just suspect an affair?"

"Oh, sure," she said, waving her hand as if that weren't important. "But when large sums of unaccounted for cash started showing up in Tom's bank account, that's when I knew something was off. And I had an officer I trust discreetly investigate for me. I can't say much about it, as it's an ongoing investigation, but I can tell you that Lucas King is being released with no charges against him. His shop will be off-limits for a week or two while we collect evidence, but other than that, he should be fine."

Hope nearly collapsed onto the table in sheer relief. But there were things she still didn't understand. "Can you at least tell me how Lucas's shop ended up being the supplier of the drug?"

"I think that would be okay since you're likely to piece it together once you see Lucas anyway," she said with a smile. "Tom stopped by one day to buy a side table—"

"Right," Hope said with a nod. "Lucas said Tom's

company could deal with his sawdust. They were going to make something out of it." Hope's eyes went wide. "Ashe?"

She nodded. "Only the sawdust needed to be treated with the magically enhanced solution and dried for a few days before they picked it up. So Tom arranged to have the drug delivered to Lucas's shop in liquid form. Lucas then 'treated' his sawdust, and one of Tom's drivers showed up to haul it away and turn it into little pellets for people to smoke. It was quite ingenious except that he was too stupid to hide his antics from me. Now here we are."

"That's... wow," Hope said, sitting back in her chair. "And Yasmeen is the ringleader?"

"Something like that." She stood. "That's all I can say for now. Besides, I think someone is waiting for you." The mayor nodded to someone over Hope's shoulder.

Hope spun around and spotted a very tired Lucas waiting for her. She sprang up from the chair and ran out of the room and into his arms.

"Damn, aren't you a sight for sore eyes," he said, breathing her in.

"You, too. I was so worried when Joy told me you'd been arrested, and then we sat here for hours waiting to tell them what Mom gleaned from Yasmeen's thoughts. I wasn't sure if we were going to get you out of here tonight or not."

He ran his hand through her dark curls, still just holding on to her. "You didn't think I'd turned into a drug lord, did you?"

She hesitated, not sure what to say.

Lucas pulled back and stared down at her, his eyes troubled. "Hope?"

"No. Not really. I mean, I *know* you. So in my heart, I really didn't. But for a few moments there, I was thrown.

And it was moving through your store, even if you didn't realize it."

"The very idea of that stuff running through my shop..." He let out a growl of frustration. "It makes me want to punch something... or someone."

She placed one hand on his cheek. "If it makes you feel better, Peggy Pitsman tried to beat the shit out of Yasmeen."

He blinked and then threw his head back and laughed. "You're kidding, right?"

"Nope. It was glorious. I'm pretty sure Peggy won."

Still chuckling, he grabbed her by the hand and said, "You're going to need to give me the blow-by-blow on the way home."

"Sure thing," she said, smiling up at him, grateful that she'd been able to make him laugh.

"Angela, do you mind if Hope sleeps over at my place tonight?" Lucas asked her mom, who was trailing them out of the station.

"Not at all. Just make sure she has coffee in the morning, or your post-coital haze will leave a little something to be desired. You know how Hope is without her caffeine."

"Ignore her," Hope demanded. "And never ask her for permission for me to sleep over again. I'm a grown-ass woman. I make my own decisions."

"Of course you do," he said with a nod. "I was just making it clear you're not coming home tonight. We have plans." Then he picked her up in one fluid motion and carried her over to her SUV. "Who's driving? Me or you?"

Hope gave him a wry smile. "Looks like you're already in the driver's seat."

"It does, doesn't it?" He nuzzled her neck and carried her over to the passenger side. After placing her in her seat, he ran around to the other side and climbed in. "Where's your mom? Doesn't she need a ride?"

Hope twisted and spotted her mom already getting into Joy's car. "Looks like she's covered. Let's go. I want nothing more than to climb into the shower with you."

Lucas nodded once, put the truck into gear, and flew out of the parking lot like the backend was on fire.

"Someone's eager," she teased.

"Hope, I just got out of jail. I have time to make up for," he said.

"Oh? Sounds like I'm in for a wild ride."

"Is that a challenge?"

She grinned at him. "You bet your ass it is."

"What do you say we get married this spring?" Lucas said to Hope as he idly toyed with her fingers while they sat in the swing on his back porch the next morning.

Hope, who'd been taking a sip of the most delicious coffee she'd ever tasted, sputtered. "What?"

"Spring? Wedding? You in a white dress? Me in a tux? Or if you prefer, we can do something casual down by the beach. Just you, me, our moms, and the coven. I'm not picky, just as long as I finally get to call you my wife."

Hope gaped at him. Then she shook her head in amazement. "Seriously? After all this time, *that's* how you propose to me?"

"What? Were you expecting some grand gesture or something? Like a string quartet, or a thousand sunflowers, or maybe something more lowkey like a gourmet breakfast for just the two of us while I get down on one knee and offer you a three-carat diamond ring?"

"Yeah. Something like that," she grumbled, eyeing his two labs who were playing and rolling around in the grass. "It's a thousand times better than 'Hey, Hope, what do you say we get married?' I mean, come on. I know I don't require a ton of romance but—"

Hope stopped talking when Lucas pulled a small blue-velvet box out of his pocket and sank down on one knee. He gave her that cocky half smile that she loved so much and opened the box. She glanced down at the ring and squinted. The sun reflecting off the giant rock nearly blinded her. "Ohmigod. Is this really happening?"

"It's really happening, Hope. I've lost you twice now because we both needed something the other couldn't give in those moments. But you know what they say about the third time being the charm."

She let out a small chuckle and wiped at the tears rolling down her cheeks. "I've heard the theory before."

"I've loved you since I was seventeen years old. It may have taken us thirty years to finally get here, but now that we are, I don't want to waste another day." He reached for her left hand and said, "Hope Anderson, will you make me the happiest man in the world and be my wife?"

"Yes," she practically shouted and then slid down to her knees and launched herself at him, kissing him with everything she had.

When they finally came up for air, he let out a throaty laugh. "Did you want this? Or should I just wait until the wedding day?"

She glanced down at the ring box in his hand and chuckled. "Yes. I want it. But I wanted to kiss you more."

"And that's just one of the reasons I love you." He winked at her and slid the shiny rock on her finger. "Come on," he said, tugging her to her feet.

"Where are we going?" she asked, unable to tear her gaze away from the antique engagement ring on her finger. It was perfect, exactly what she'd have picked out herself.

"Breakfast." He led her back into the house where there was an elaborate spread of breakfast food on the table.

She glanced at the plates of pancakes, croissants, eggs, bacon, and toast. Fresh orange juice sat next to a plate of blueberry muffins, making Hope throw her head back and laugh. It was exactly like the breakfast scene in *Pretty Woman*. Every time they'd had breakfast together when they were dating, she'd say a gentleman would order everything on the menu for his woman just like Edward Lewis did for Vivian. Hope turned and wrapped her arms around him. "I can't believe you remembered."

"Baby, I remember everything." He dipped his head and claimed her mouth, making her breathless.

"Get a room," Lucas's mother called from the kitchen doorway.

Hope pulled back just enough to poke her head around his shoulder to look at her and wave her left hand in her direction. "Did you know about this, Bell?"

"Absolutely. Who do you think helped him pick out the ring?" She winked and added, "Congratulations. Now, seriously, get a room. A woman has things to do around here."

Laughing, Lucas scooped her up and did exactly that, making her forget all about her *Pretty Woman* breakfast.

CHAPTER TWENTY-NINE

"That's going to be you soon," Joy told Hope as they sat in white chairs on the bluff watching Skyler and Pete walk their two shih tzus down the aisle. Polly was dressed in a billowy white satin gown, and Drew was wearing the most adorable checked vest with a matching bow tie. It was enough to make a girl melt from the sheer cuteness.

"Please. I'm going to be wearing a bikini top and a sarong, and Lucas is gonna be in board shorts," Hope insisted.

Joy rolled her eyes. "Not if Bell and Angela have anything to say about it."

Hope sighed, and Joy knew her friend was going to cave. Angela and Bell both had thought they'd never see the day come when their kids would get married. They were desperate to be part of the celebration. Hope wouldn't deny them that, no matter how much she wanted to run away and elope with the man of her dreams. "You'd think it'd be easier planning it, considering that's what I do for a living. But every time I think about it, I just don't care. The only thing I want is to actually be married to him."

It was Joy's turn to sigh. She'd been that woman once many years ago when she and Paul were engaged. Joy hadn't cared about the ceremony either. All she wanted was to start her life with the man she was head over heels for. Too bad he'd walked out almost thirty years later, the jackass. Now she was starting over and a little bit lost. She needed a job that was more significant than volunteer at the Arts Market.

She also needed a date. And as much as she talked about trying out the Tinder app, she wasn't really up for meeting some stranger from the internet. Whatever happened to meeting people in person and hitting it off?

"It's a little crazy isn't it?" a man's voice asked from beside her.

Joy jumped slightly, not having realized someone had taken the seat next to her. "Damn, Troy. When did you get here?" she whispered to the tall, lanky man with the kind blue eyes. She let her gaze travel over his torso, and she couldn't help wondering what was hiding beneath his perfectly pressed white button-down shirt.

"Just now. I'm glad I didn't miss the vows. How do they do it? Bark at each other? Share a treat? Sniff each other's nether regions?"

Joy had to stifle a giggle that earned her dirty looks from the people in the row in front of them. "Thanks a lot," she whispered to him. "Now I'm not going to be invited to their silver anniversary party."

"I'm sure you'll be forgiven by then. If not, you can enjoy the day at the beach or spa or in my hot tub instead." He gave her a sexy little smile that made her insides wake up and say hello.

He was flirting with her. Oh, gods. Did she remember how to flirt? How long had it been since an attractive man had shown interest in her? She couldn't remember. Hell, she couldn't even remember the last time she'd had sex, much less anything else.

"You're missing it," he said, nudging her arm.

"Missing what?" she asked and then quickly realized that the ceremony was over, and Pete and Skyler were carrying their precious little puppies back down the aisle and inviting everyone over to their beach house for a reception.

"Well, glad it didn't last all day," Troy said. "Can I walk you over to the party?"

"Sure." Joy glanced over at Hope and Lucas, intending to let them know she'd see them there, but they were already chatting with Iris Hartsen. It sounded like they were getting the scoop on how her husband had managed a plea deal to avoid jail time, but no deal had worked on Iris. The moment he was bailed out of jail, she'd thrown him out. *And good for her,* Joy thought. No woman needed a man she couldn't trust.

She turned her attention back to Troy and slipped her arm through his. "I'll catch them later. Let's go."

They walked by themselves down the oceanfront road toward Skyler and Pete's house. But before they got there, Troy stopped in front of a large modern home that had windows for days. "I forgot the gift. Want to come inside while I grab it?"

"Do I? Of course I do. I don't think I've ever seen a house this gorgeous before. It must be tiring to stare at that view all the time," she teased.

His lips curved into a ghost of a smile. "You know how it is. Someone had to, so it might as well be me."

"Poor guy. I feel for you."

He led her into the house, and instead of it being stark white like she expected, the walls were painted a warm taupe and had photography covering almost every available vertical surface. Which admittedly was lacking considering all of the windows, but it was still impressive.

While Troy went off to find his wedding gift, Joy got lost in the prints on his wall. There was one in particular of a woman wrapped in a silk sheet looking disheveled and completely ravished that she just could not tear her eyes from. She was so powerful in her sexuality that Joy couldn't help but be a little jealous.

"You know, you're even more beautiful than that model," Troy said. "I'd love to shoot you sometime. You'd make a great subject."

The thought excited her. She'd modeled when she was younger for a bit before she'd married Paul, and she even had aspirations to be an actress for a while. But that had been too long ago. Joy turned to eye him and asked, "Are you serious? Because that sounded more like a proposition than a modeling offer."

He tilted his head to the side and narrowed his eyes slightly. "Yes, I was serious. I hire models all the time. I pay the going rate. Think about it and let me know, okay?"

"Yeah, Okay."

"But I'm curious. Why did that sound like a proposition?"

She shrugged. "It's just that this woman has so obviously just been ravished. And by the way she's looking at the camera, I'm certain that the two of you had just..." She waved a hand. "You know."

His eyebrows shot up. "No. What?"

Her mouth went dry, and she suddenly wondered what

had possessed her to bring this up. "You know. Sex. You two just had sex."

"We did?" His eyes crinkled with amusement.

"Are you trying to tell me you didn't?" she demanded, placing her hands on her hips.

"That's exactly what I'm saying."

"I don't believe you." Joy shook her head. "There's just no way."

He nodded thoughtfully. "I can see why you think that. It's obvious this photographer has a relationship with his subject. The only problem with your theory is that I didn't shoot this picture. A friend of mine did. This woman was his lover at the time. They're now married. I bought this print because it reminds me that love should be full of passion and fire and heat and everything that lights a person up from the inside. I want that one day. Don't you?"

Joy's breath left her. And just like that, his words made her want to throw herself at him. She placed a hand on his chest, stared him in the eyes, and whispered, "Yes. More than anything."

He didn't hesitate. Troy moved in and claimed her mouth with his. The kiss was full of fire and intense need. Joy stepped into him, wrapping her arms around his muscled shoulders, and just sank into everything he had to offer.

When they finally broke apart, Troy's eyes were full of want, something she hadn't seen in far too long when a man looked at her.

"Dammit, Joy. I want you. Badly," he said. "Would it be too forward to ask you to share the afternoon with me in my bed?"

They stared at each other for what seemed like forever as the electricity sparked between them. And even though he'd offered her a modeling job, and it was undoubtedly unprofessional to sleep with the photographer, there was nothing in the entire universe that could stop her from saying yes to his proposition.

Because it was definitely time Joy got her groove back.

DEANNA'S BOOK LIST

Witches of Keating Hollow:
Soul of the Witch
Heart of the Witch
Spirit of the Witch
Dreams of the Witch
Courage of the Witch
Love of the Witch
Power of the Witch
Essence of the Witch
Muse of the Witch
Vision of the Witch

Witches of Christmas Grove:
A Witch For Mr. Holiday
A Witch For Mr. Christmas

Premonition Pointe Novels:
Witching For Grace
Witching For Hope

Witching For Joy

Jade Calhoun Novels:
Haunted on Bourbon Street
Witches of Bourbon Street
Demons of Bourbon Street
Angels of Bourbon Street
Shadows of Bourbon Street
Incubus of Bourbon Street
Bewitched on Bourbon Street
Hexed on Bourbon Street
Dragons of Bourbon Street

Pyper Rayne Novels:
Spirits, Stilettos, and a Silver Bustier
Spirits, Rock Stars, and a Midnight Chocolate Bar
Spirits, Beignets, and a Bayou Biker Gang
Spirits, Diamonds, and a Drive-thru Daiquiri Stand
Spirits, Spells, and Wedding Bells

Ida May Chronicles:
Witched To Death
Witch, Please
Stop Your Witchin'

Crescent City Fae Novels:
Influential Magic
Irresistible Magic
Intoxicating Magic

Last Witch Standing:
Bewitched by Moonlight

Soulless at Sunset
Bloodlust By Midnight
Bitten At Daybreak

Witch Island Brides:
The Wolf's New Year Bride
The Vampire's Last Dance
The Warlock's Enchanted Kiss
The Shifter's First Bite

Destiny Novels:
Defining Destiny
Accepting Fate

Wolves of the Rising Sun:
Jace
Aiden
Luc
Craved
Silas
Darien
Wren

Black Bear Outlaws:
Cyrus
Chase
Cole

Bayou Springs Alien Mail Order Brides:
Zeke
Gunn
Echo

ABOUT THE AUTHOR

New York Times and USA Today bestselling author, Deanna Chase, is a native Californian, transplanted to the slower paced lifestyle of southeastern Louisiana. When she isn't writing, she is often goofing off with her husband in New Orleans or playing with her two shih tzu dogs. For more information and updates on newest releases visit her website at deannachase.com.

Made in the USA
Middletown, DE
01 April 2021